THE FACE OF THE STRANGER

Fashion photographer Rane had taken
against Greville York from the very
first moment she met him at Leo
d'Arvel's Spring Collection—so she
was dismayed to find that her next
assignment would be at Greville's
house! And if Greville thought he was
going to prevent his young ward
Marion marrying Leo, then Rane was
going to do all she could to thwart him!

THE FACE OF THE STRANGER

BY

ANGELA CARSON

MILLS & BOON LIMITED
15–16 BROOK'S MEWS
LONDON W1A 1DR

First published 1983
Australian copyright 1983
Philippine copyright 1983
This edition 1983

© Angela Carson 1983

ISBN 0 263 74405 1

Set in Monophoto Plantin 10 on 11 pt.
01–1183 – 53817

Made and printed in Great Britain by
Richard Clay (The Chaucer Press) Ltd,
Bungay, Suffolk

CHAPTER ONE

THE face of the stranger!

It stared back at her from the photographic proof, hatchet-cut, rock-jawed, not at all the type of face she expected to catch in her camera lens in a Paris fashion salon during the showing of Leo d'Arvel's exotic Spring Collection.

'I loathe you!' Rane scowled down at the face. It glared back at her with equal ferocity, mirroring the glare it gave her in the salon, and plainly reciprocating her own feelings of hearty dislike at first sight. If anything, the stranger's well-cut lips seemed to increase their satirical upwards twist as she looked at him, scorning her opinion of him as obviously as he scorned the perfumed world of high fashion into which, with a face like his, Rane decided critically, he could only have strayed by the merest chance. A diabolical chance, so far as she herself was concerned.

'It's a super picture, but hardly what you went all the way to Paris for. That is, unless he's a boy-friend of yours?' Clive Redman, the magazine's editor, perched interestedly on the edge of Rane's desk and gave her a quizzical look.

'I didn't go to Paris to get a picture of *him*, you idiot! And he's not my boy-friend,' Rane denied emphatically. The face staring back at her was not a boy's face. It was that of a man, lean, strong. And curiously disturbing. Rane gave herself a mental shake and averted her eyes, but against her will they returned to the pictured face, drawn by a strange magnetism that she could not explain, and discovered she did not particularly want to think about.

'The man's a menace!' She did not add, to her own peace of mind. Uneasily she thrust the thought away, but for some reason her fingers refused to thrust away the picture as well. They clung to the print with a stubbornness that was unnerving, and she carried on speaking hastily, lest Clive should comment on their strange attachment. 'He stood up just as I was about to get a shot of that stunning evening gown. He completely spoiled my picture.' She scowled malevolently at the stranger's face. 'That evening gown with the butterfly motifs was a magnificent creation, the best in Leo's Collection. The skirt flowed outwards in a perfect fan, and with a hint of blur to give it movement, it would have made a super picture. And that idiot had to choose the crucial moment to stand up right in front of me and spoil the best shot of the evening! And then he had the effrontery to blame *me* for pointing my camera at *him*!' she remembered indignantly.

'Don't aim your camera at me.' He did not bother to raise his voice. Even above the hubbub in the salon, it had a curious carrying quality, that flicked across the crowded room like a whiplash, demanding, commanding, expecting to be obeyed. For a second or two her eyes had remained glued to the viewfinder on her camera, expecting the stranger to move out of her range of vision. When he remained where he was, glaring back at her, she waved an impatient hand for him to move to one side, but instead of moving his response was an angry,

'Don't aim your camera at me!'

It could only be herself he spoke to. Hers was the only camera allowed at the showing. No one else was even allowed to make sketches of the Collection, let alone take photographs, and the stranger stood blocking her view of Leo's pièce de résistance, with apparently no intention of moving out of her line of vision.

'You've ruined my shot!' she condemned him furiously.

'Good. That will effectively prevent you from trying to publish it,' the stranger retorted crisply, and Rane stared at him in sheer disbelief.

'I travelled all the way to Paris for the express purpose of publishing whatever photographs I take,' she spluttered furiously. 'Why else do you think I'm here?' she demanded.

'A woman's reasons for being anywhere are usually as devious as they're self-deceiving.' No spark of humour lightened the cold steel grey of his eyes, that bored into her own from under uncompromisingly straight brows as black as his short cropped hair—as black as the scowl that drew his brows into an intimidating line. 'But just in case your picture should turn out to be recognisable, make sure it's not printed,' he warned her sternly.

'I won't be told by you what I must and must not print,' Rane hotly asserted her freedom to do as she chose. 'I'll publish whatever I think fit!'

'You won't publish a photograph of me.'

His tone, his whole bearing, held an undeniable menace, and momentarily Rane caught her breath, and with it a resurgence of courage. The arrogance of the man! He had stood up, right in front of her camera, and then had the conceit to imagine she was pointing it at him, and not at the models on the catwalks!

'How arrogant of you to assume I wanted a picture of you, and not of the models.' By a supreme effort of will she made her voice coolly sarcastic, thrusting aside her artistic instinct that insisted the fine, aristocratic features confronting her would make a perfect subject for a dramatic portrait. The features tightened at her words, and the steely eyes narrowed into glinting slits.

'Whatever your reason for photographing me, make sure the results aren't published,' he reiterated curtly.

'Why, what have you got to hide?' Rane flashed back, and wondered at herself even as she spoke. Despite her arresting colouring of sea green eyes and copper hair, and a fiery spirit to match, she was not usually rude to perfect strangers. This one proved to be the exception. With an acquaintance only seconds old, he succeeded in bringing out the very worst in her.

'I have my own reasons for not revealing my presence here to members of the gutter press.' He did not attempt to hide his dislike of herself, and Rane's eyes widened at the deliberate insult. Gutter press, indeed! The man was insufferable. She opened her mouth to tell him so, and closed it again with a snap as he neatly forestalled her with,

'So you can inform the editor of whatever rag you represent that if any picture of me appears on his front page, I'll sue him.'

Again, the overweening arrogance, to assume that whatever other world-shattering events might be taking place at the time, his picture would make front page news.

'You're insufferable!'

He was no longer there. Rane vented her spleen on empty air. With a quickness that took her unawares, he delivered his parting shot, spun on his heel, and melted into the crowd with a dexterity that she hated herself for envying. From bitter experience she knew that her diminutive stature, burdened as it was with photographic hardware, would make her own progress through the packed room an exhausting struggle. It was impossible to discover where the stranger had gone to. She stood on tiptoe, but her lack of inches prevented her from seeing over the heads of the crowd as it rose with one accord to pay homage to the brilliance of the designer.

'Bravo! Bravo!'

The audience was on its feet, applauding its approval of Leo's creations, and Rane felt a quick glow at the young Frenchman's undoubted success. He was young, an unknown on the fashion scene, and this, his first major showing, could make or break him. Across the fickle sky of the fashion world, many such meteorites flashed and died with monotonous regularity, and Rane felt an immense satisfaction that the highly strung, immensely likeable young designer, who invaded her office at the magazine's headquarters and dropped his proposal like a bombshell across her cluttered desk, was now receiving the ovation his undoubted talents deserved.

'Photograph the first showing of your Spring Collection, for publication in *Dress*? You must be mad! Cameras are an anathema to fashion designers.' She voiced her amazement at his suggestion. 'Why, even the fashion experts aren't allowed to sketch a collection during the first showing, let alone take photographs. And you actually want a preview of yours published?' she asked Leo incredulously.

'*Dress* is hardly a normal publication.' The young, sensitive face, with the high, intelligent forehead, became thoughtful. 'It's an exclusive, international, subscription-only magazine, is it not?' Rane nodded. 'So,' her visitor continued, thrusting home his point, 'it will reach the very clientele for whom I design my clothes. Women of discernment. . . .'

'And wealth,' Rane put in drily.

'And wealth,' Leo laughed, and then sobered. '*Dress* comes out four times a year, to meet the few fashion seasons. I'll time the showing of my Collection to coincide with the publication of your next issue. Your subscribers will receive their magazine within twenty-four hours of the buyers and fashion experts seeing the Collection, and who knows, they might attend the next showing themselves.'

'What about security?' Rane asked him bluntly. Plagiarism, or to put it more crudely, industrial espionage, was an ever-present threat lurking beneath the flowered and perfumed surface of the fashion scene, and stringent precautions were necessary to protect the details of each new design until the time was ripe for it to be presented to a startled world. The slightest carelessness could lead to wholesale copying, and represent wasted months of work, and possible financial ruin for the unlucky designer. Her newfound acquaintance was young, and obviously naïve as well, Rane decided pityingly.

'Security insurance would be written into the contract between us.'

He was not so naïve as Rane imagined. Beneath his artistic exterior lurked a shrewd business sense, and she regarded her visitor with new respect.

'It's still an unusual idea.' But it was one that could be made to work, if Leo was willing to take the risk, she acknowledged with dawning interest.

'My designs are unusual, but they're already creating interest.'

It was no empty boast, as the showing of his Collection proved. Rane arrived early, and the sight of her camera, carried openly with no hint of conceal-ment, brought some startled looks in her direction. Within minutes of the commencement of the showing, the atmosphere of polite interest in the salon turned to an alert awareness that here was something different. Another five minutes, and the room became charged with an electric excitement which infected Rane to a degree that nearly made her forget her camera, and simply gape open-mouthed at the clothes passing in front of her eyes.

Gay clothes. Desirable clothes. Clothes that appealed to those with flair and a sense of the unusual, but—and here Leo's sound business sense was once more in evidence—clothes that manufacturers could eventually translate into ready-to-wear garments suitable for the High Street shops. One after the other the mannequins skilfully drew attention to dramatic collars, emphatic waists, sleek suits, and soft, utterly feminine dresses that made Rane's mouth water, and her own wardrobe seem dowdy and out of date by comparison.

Leo was clever. The mood of his collection was young, the clothes chic and fabulously expensive, but at the same time eminently wearable. The tempo of the showing was fast, the mannequins criss-crossing one another briskly on the X-shaped platform, and Rane was kept busy taking as many shots as possible of each outfit until, with an instinct of pure showmanship, Leo followed two severely cut evening gowns with the final model of his collection, an exquisite ball dress in delphinium blue silk.

The high shawl collar fell into a wide sash, both liberally embroidered with beads and sequins in a delicate butterfly motif, that glittered in the lights as the mannequin pirouetted for the benefit of her audience. Rane gave a gasp of pure delight, that was echoed across the room, and managed three quick shots as the girl stepped daintily to the centre of the catwalk, where she paused, and with the grace of a ballerina swayed and dipped, so that the layered skirt of the gown sighed outwards from her slender waist, softly audible like the whisper of shared dreams. The dress was every woman's dream. Eagerly Rane's finger pressed the shutter for the fourth time, just as the stranger stood up.

'Bravo! Bravo!'

It was too late now. The stranger was gone, and so was the mannequin. Midnight blue velvet curtains fell across the stage, and Leo appeared through them to receive the applause that was his due. Rane saw with amusement that he was dressed in a suit of the same dark blue velvet. Again, the hint of showmanship was evident. The deep blue suited his blond colouring and gaunt good looks, and made it his individual colour, along with the blue velvet-and-gilt chairs, and the blue carpet in the salon.

'The Wedgwood touch,' Rane murmured appreciatively. She would use it as a caption in her write-up. Names tended to catch on. But in the meantime, her photograph was more important.

'Perhaps I can catch the mannequin before she gets changed, and persuade her to pose for me.' The other photographs she had taken of the gown would suffice, but the last, the one she had missed because of the stranger, was something special. She glanced at her watch. 'I'll have to hurry,' she muttered anxiously. To catch the printing deadline of the magazine, she had to be on the evening plane to London. Twenty minutes to photograph the dress, and then a quick dash across Paris in a taxi. . . . But haste was impossible in the crowded room. Rane had not the advantage of the stanger's six foot plus of athletic masculinity to save her from being buffeted by the crush of humanity, and she was hot and breathless by the time she gained the entrance to the mannequins' dressing room behind the small stage.

'Marion?' To her relief the young mannequin who had modelled the dress was still there. So was the stranger. Rane's relief vanished. 'What on earth is he doing behind the scenes?' she muttered irritably. It was the last place she expected to find him. To make matters worse, he was engaged in conversation with the young mannequin as if they were on familiar terms. Rane's lip curled. The stranger had an eye for a pretty face, and evidently a liking for ultra-young company. If nothing else, it explained his reason for being in the salon in the first place. Marion was the youngest of Leo's mannequins. Rane had met her briefly before the showing of the Collection, and at eighteen she must be at least twelve, if not more, years younger than the stranger.

'Cradle-snatching!' Rane muttered scornfully, and lost her reluctance to interrupt the pair. Marion had already changed into a cocktail dress, ready to join the reception which was getting under way in the salon, but the ball gown was still in evidence, being carefully folded in tissue wraps by the elderly dresser.

'Sorry to interrupt you, Marion.' Rane was not sorry. She was probably doing the young girl a favour, she decided scathingly. Eighteen-year-old mannequins were no different from other teenagers, in that they were just as prone to being dazzled by the prosperous, man-of-the-world air that sat on the stranger so easily as did his faultlessly tailored clothes.

'Marion and I are talking.'

A lesser spirit would have wilted under his unwelcoming frown. The force of it made Rane blink, but she stood her ground, and called on her copper curls to quell the uneasy fluttering that for no good reason suddenly disturbed her normally well controlled interior, which reacted to the stranger's closer proximity in a manner that assailed her mind with the same sense of unease. Impatiently she thrust it away. She did not know what unlikely chance brought the stranger here, but she, Rane, had an unassailable right to attend the showing, and time was too pressing to allow anything, or anybody, to stand in the way of her obtaining her coveted photograph. With a defiant tilt of her chin she asserted her right, and asked confidently.

'Will you change back into the ball gown and pose for me, Marion? When you dipped to the floor, and the skirt flowed out round you, it made a perfect picture, but an inconsiderate member of the audience stood up right in front of me just as I pressed the shutter, and completely spoiled my shot.' Unrepentantly she allowed the culprit to know just how inconsiderate she thought his behaviour was. Maliciously she rubbed in the fact that she had aimed her camera at the ball gown, and not at him.

'No one but a gnome could possibly sit on one of those ghastly chairs for more than ten minutes without doing his spine a permanent injury,' the stranger growled unexpectedly, and sudden mirth bubbled up in Rane. So sheer discomfort was the reason he had jumped to his feet so suddenly! She knew what he meant about the chairs. 'All looks, and no comfort,' one disgruntled fashion editor called the seemingly inevitable item of all fashion salon furnishing, and his description could hardly be bettered. Rane savoured the thought of the stranger's wriggling agony before desperation ejected him from his seat. It almost made the lost photograph worth while. Almost. . . .

'Marion hasn't time to change again. She's coming with me.'

He quelled the mirth and brought back the angry frustration, and Rane flushed furiously at his peremptory tone.

'Marion can decide for herself.' She hotly contested his right to interfere.

'We're scheduled to take off in under the hour.' The stranger pushed up a flawless white shirt cuff and consulted a wafer-thin gold watch, directing his remark to Marion as if Rane had not spoken.

'Marion?' Rane took a leaf out of the stranger's book, and did exactly the same thing, trying unsuccessfully to stifle the qualm that went through her at his words. Her own flight left in under the hour. It would be the last straw if some evil mischance put the stranger on the same plane as herself. Perhaps— her mind boggled at the possibility—perhaps even in the next seat to herself.

'Marion?' The thought was not to be borne, and she urged it away with her plea to the young mannequin.

'I've already told you——' the stranger began harshly, when Marion broke in, her young voice strained.

'I can't come with you, Greville.' She was actually refusing him! Rane wanted to cheer. Not many people would have the temerity, and plainly he was not accustomed to his orders being disobeyed. Rane sent the newly named Greville a triumphant glance, and the desire to cheer died within her. Devil would be a better name for him, she thought with a shocked intake of breath. Tightly controlled fury moulded his face into an expression of rocklike hardness, and the look in his eyes boded ill for Marion if she should continue to defy him. Surely suitors were supposed to plead their cause to the lady of their choice? Not so the stranger. Intuition told Rane he would never plead. He would invade, and capture, and lay down his own terms. . . .

'I've simply *got* to go to the reception, Greville. Leo expects all his mannequins to be there.'

'—Leo!'

Evidently the stranger saw a rival in the young designer. Rane's amusement returned, accompanied by an odd sense of relief. Relief for Marion, of course. It *had* to be for Marion. There could be no other possible reason for her, Rane, to feel such an overwhelming sense of relief. It left her slightly dizzy. She had only met Marion briefly before the showing of the Collection, but she had taken an instant liking to the attractive teenager, with her short-cropped fair hair and tall, lissom model's figure that was nearly three inches taller than Rane's own diminutive measurements. Leo was much nearer to Marion's age, and altogether more suitable. Rane hoped the girl would have the good sense to fix her sights on the designer, and not be bowled over by the more mature attraction of the stranger.

'I sound like a matchmaking dowager,' Rane told herself scornfully. 'And anyway, who called Greville whatever-his-name-is attractive?' She had. And she did not want to dwell upon the unpalatable fact, that her photographer's eye told her was a blatant understatement. Marion effectively put an end to her dwelling upon it, by imploring.

'Why don't you join us at the reception, Greville? Surely another hour wouldn't make all that much difference?' It obviously would, if the stranger was booked on the evening flight, but to an eager eighteen-year-old, beckoned by a glittering reception, probably her first, what did a missed flight matter? 'You could meet Leo, talk to him. . . .'

'I've seen all I need to of Leo,' the stranger snarled, and Rane's eyes widened at the venom in his voice. Inconceivable though it might seem, the man was actually jealous of the young designer, Rane deduced, and he did not seem to care who knew it. He proceeded to voice his feelings in no uncertain terms. 'The man's hair's twice the length of yours,' he condemned the absent Leo. 'And that velvet suit,' he snorted, 'all he needs is a lace collar to turn him into a perfect Little Lord Fauntleroy. The man's a positive. . . .'

'*Monsieur!*'

The elderly dresser's ample frame was stiff with disapproval, her mein reminiscent of a nursery governess as she bore down upon them, the ball gown rustling in its layers of tissue paper over her arm.

'Greville, I must fly—I really must. Leo will be wondering where on earth I've got to.' And from a situation that was patently too much for her, Marion fled. The dresser gave the stranger a quelling glance and followed in her wake, taking with her Rane's last hope of the desired photograph and leaving her, for the second time that afternoon, face to face with the stranger. Her wrath spilled over.

'If you hadn't interfered, I'd have got my photograph, and been half way to the airport by now!'

'If you hadn't so rudely interrupted our conversation, so would I,' he retorted, and added grimly, 'and Marion would have been with me.'

'Not necessarily. Marion's quite old enough to know her own mind,' Rane replied sharply. She would not be held to blame for the girl's choice. In fact, it was one in which she heartily concurred. 'Thanks to you, I've probably missed my flight as well as my photograph,' she flung over her shoulder as her heels tapped an angry tattoo on the unglamorous linoleum-covered backstage corridor leading to the exit. She did not know if the stranger heard her or not, and by now she did not care. A dismayed glance at her watch gave her more immediate problems to worry about than

what his reaction might be to her remark. Her flight
left in less than twenty-five minutes.

'Thanks to you, I've probably missed my own
schedule!' she added crossly.

Disconcertingly, he was just behind her, his soft-
soled shoes making no sound on the hard surface of
the floor, and her heartbeats quickened to match her
steps. She tried to excuse her haste on the need to
reach the airport in time to catch her flight, but a
peculiar breathlessness made hurrying difficult, and
the stranger reached the door ahead of her. His hand
grasped the knob, and Rane paused, nonplussed. Was
he going to bar her way and deliberately delay her so
that she should miss her flight? She raised an angry
face, and her green eyes flashed sparks as they met his.

'Allow me.' His mocking glance read her suspicions
with ease, jeered at her for entertaining them, and for
the uncertainty that provoked her breathlessness.
Long, slender fingers, the fingers of an artist or a
musician, wrenched at the knob, and he flung the door
wide and with a gesture invited her to step through.
With a set face, Rane stepped. She heard the door
close, and only by exerting every ounce of willpower
did she prevent herself from glancing behind her to
see if the stranger followed her out. The next second
she did not need to look back. Her spine tingled with
the knowledge that he was still there, only a pace
behind her, some indefinable aura announcing his
presence with a certainty she could not ignore. A knot
of nerves tightened at the back of her neck, in a
manner that threatened to become a splitting headache
later, and she drew in a deep breath of damp
November air in a desperate attempt to subdue the
uneasy flutterings of her stomach, that returned with
full force and threatened to outdo her rapidly
accelerating heartbeats for discomfort.

The cold air steadied her, and two things impinged
on her consciousness. One was the small group of
men, three in number, who stood waiting on the edge
of the pavement, and the second was the solitary taxi
cruising among the sparse traffic on the street, and on
which the attention of the group was fixed.

'Taxi!'

No matter what the needs of the unknown group,
her own need was paramount. She *must* reach London
with her film on time to meet the magazine's printing
deadline.

'Taxi!'

The stranger stepped from behind her, his hand
upraised in a signal to the driver, and to Rane's
chagrin passed the group of strangers, passed herself,
and came to a halt with the driver's door within inches
of the stranger's feet.

'I hailed the taxi first,' she began furiously.

'We were here before you were, miss.'

The situation looked like becoming unpleasant.
Rane gave a desperate glance along the street, but
there was no other taxi in sight, in either direction.

'I must. . . .' she began urgently.

'Leave this to me.' The stranger waved her to
silence with an imperious hand, and went on in suave
tones, 'If, as I suspect, we're all heading for the same
destination, it seems to me sensible that we all share
the same taxi.'

'We're going to the airport.'

'And so are we.'

The effrontery of the man, to couple her with
himself! He made it sound as if they were travelling
together. Rane stiffened resentfully, and instantly, as if
he sensed her instinctive refusal to comply, the
stranger's hand closed round her elbow and propelled
her willy-nilly towards the cab door.

'Ladies first. That is, unless you want to miss your flight?' he taunted her sotto voce.

It was a mistake to allow him to touch her. The second his hand grasped her elbow, a sensation like a lightning bolt burned through her arm and set it tingling to the very ends of her fingers. Bemusedly Rane wondered if the heat of it might fuse the delicate mechanism of her camera, and then, hardly conscious of what she was doing, she found herself climbing meekly into the roomy back of the taxi, stumbling on legs that had become oddly paralysed, unlike her arm which the stranger no longer held, but which felt vibrantly, exhilaratingly alive.

He got in last, and sat opposite to her on one of the small pull-down seats. With a catch of her breath that was more of a sob than a laugh, Rane wondered if he would find it as uncomfortable as the gilt and velvet chair in the salon. Mischievous hope rose in her that he would, that he would be forced, this time, to endure the discomfort, because there was nowhere for him to go if he tried to stand up, unless he exchanged seats with the grossly overweight individual who sat next to her, and who appeared intent on crushing her into the corner of the taxi until she felt she was being moulded into its shape. She glanced up, and her cheeks warmed. Cool grey eyes appraised her discomfort, lighting with a sudden flare of laughter that assured her her uncharitable wish was not to be granted, that he found his seat supremely comfortable, and viewed with amusement the knowledge that she would have to endure her own squashed state until the taxi reached their destination.

The journey seemed endless. Her fellow traveller's elbow dug into her ribs on the one side, the taxi cab armrest dug into her ribs on the other, and she was bruised and breathless by the time the cab drew to a halt in front of the terminal building.

'I can manage for myself, thank you,' she refused the stranger's proffered hand in a voice as stiff as her limbs. Somehow she must force her numb legs to carry her. She dreaded the possibility that he might touch her again. She feared the contact, and scorned herself for her fear, but it did not drive it away, and she scrambled crabwise across the seat in undignified haste and reached for her purse as she was ejected on to the pavement.

'That won't be necessary.' Ice crackled in his voice.

'I'll pay my share the same as the others,' she insisted proudly.

'No lady rides with me and pays her own fare.' He accepted the group's share from the overweight man, ignored Rane's outstretched hand clutching a fan of French notes, and with a brief inclination of his head that could be interpreted as either farewell or dismissal, whichever she chose, he strode away towards the revolving doors of the terminal building and disappeared inside.

'Well!' Rane stuffed the notes back into her purse with angry fingers. 'He might have waited, and walked in with us!'

'He was in a big hurry, I guess.' The rest of her fellow passengers accompanied her through the formalities and into the departure lounge, so there was no reason why she should feel rejected. Nevertheless, the feeling persisted, a nagging sense of discontent that sent her eyes ranging round the occupants of the departure lounge before she could check their anxious searching. The stranger was not among them. Disappointment and relief fought for supremacy, and caused her to miss the gist of the announcement that twanged through a loudspeaker in a corner of the room. She raised enquiring eyebrows to the overweight member of the group.

'Seems our flight's been delayed to allow a private plane to take off first,' he explained obligingly. 'That looks as if it might be the one, over there,' he pointed through the observation window to where a sleek executive jet taxied out on to the tarmac. Minutes passed as it ran nearly out of sight, turned, and paused while the pilot revved the engine in a precautionary pre-flight check. Rane stared at it fixedly. She ought to be worrying about her own delayed flight, about meeting or missing printing deadlines, but instead she watched the silver plane as if her life depended upon it, until with a sound that reminded her irresistibly of an angry hornet, it lifted into a perfect take-off and zoomed out of sight over the building.

'Was it your friend in the plane?' The overweight one noticed her interest, and Rane felt herself go pink.

'Yes. Yes, it was.' It was too much trouble to explain that the stranger was not her friend. It was impossible to explain her conviction that it was he who was piloting the executive jet. She only knew that it was. That his slim fingers, which had so recently held her arm in a grip that made it tingle still, were the ones that held firm on the controls of the private plane, his the mind intent on the responses of the complex machine, her own image already forgotten as his eyes alternately took in the messages from his instrument panel, and raked the horizon ahead of him. Eyes that stared up at her now from the photograph she held in her fingers, with a strange, mesmeric effect that made her unable to release the oblong proof.

'Better not let my wife see these prints, or she'll want every outfit in the Collection!' Clive Redman shuffled the results of Rane's trip to Paris into a tidy pack in one large hand, and rummaged in her desk drawer for an elastic band to slip over them. 'My bank balance would never stand it,' he groaned.

'Make sure your wife doesn't see this quarter's issue of *Dress*,' Rane replied, and added absently, 'the rubber bands are in the box in the bottom drawer, not the middle one.'

'Don't be silly, my wife doesn't subscribe to *Dress*.' Its editor selected his rubber band and made to depart. 'The cost of the magazine is almost as much as the cost of Leo what's-his-name's model clothes,' he quipped.

If looking at the mere photograph of the stranger was going to have this effect on her pulse rate, the cost to herself was likely to be very much higher, Rane realised distractedly.

CHAPTER TWO

CHRISTMAS came and went, and amid the bustle of family festivities the stranger receded into the background. Receded, Rane acknowledged ruefully, but he did not disappear. He was not the type of person who allowed himself to be forgotten. To assist in the process, Rane relegated his photograph to the bottom drawer of her desk, jeering at her own lack of self-discipline that she did not instead relegate it to the shredding machine, treatment she would have meted out without a second thought if the face had belonged to anyone else.

'What a start to the New Year!'

It had brought snow, bills, and Clive Redman's invariable attack of midwinter depression.

'Cheer up. Think of the extra subscribers we've netted for *Dress* since we showed Leo d'Arvel's Spring Collection in the last issue.' Rane tried her best to cheer him up, in spite of the fact that her own spirits were as low as his.

'That's all very well, but I want something *new* for the magazine,' Clive gloomed. 'Something different, really different, not just a hotted-up version of things we've already done a dozen times before.'

'Why not go to town on the showing of Leo's Summer Collection?' Rane suggested helpfully. 'You could run a special supplement, exclusive to his designs. If it's successful, you could make it a designer's supplement, say a different designer each year. That way you'd generate a bit of competition among the fashion world, and make it a New Year

mystery as to who the next designer would be. A sort
of haute couture "This is Your Life".'

'That's an idea.' The winter weary editor brightened
visibly. 'Has d'Arvel given you a date yet for his next
showing?' he enquired interestedly.

'The end of March,' Rane replied promptly, and
tried ineffectually to stifle the craven shrinking from
the date that burned an indelible reminder in her
memory, warning her that when she put in an
appearance at the showing, so, too, might the stranger
Greville. 'Unless,' she thought hopefully, 'unless
Marion's managed to get the message across that she
doesn't want him, so he won't come after all.' And so
prevent him from reading the message in her own eyes
that if Marion did not want him, however much she
tried to persuade herself to the contrary, she, Rane,
did.

'Go away, do,' she bade Clive sharply, 'or I'll never
finish this article on Renaissance jewellery in time for
the next copy date.' She was aware of Clive's surprised
look, aware that her tone was irritable, so she added
hastily, with a forced attempt at lightheartedness she
was far from feeling, 'The women in those days
literally loaded themselves with heavy jewellery.' If
she went on like this, Rane told herself bleakly, Clive
would begin to suspect that something was amiss. And
nothing was. Nothing must be. 'It surprises me that
they could manage to walk with the weight of it hung
about them.'

Leo's telephone call that afternoon surprised her
even more.

'I hadn't expected to hear from you until the
beginning of March,' she told him.

'I need to talk to you about my Summer Collection.
Meet me for lunch at the Lighterman,' he mentioned a
small Thamesside pub that offered excellent food and

secluded inglenooks for those of its guests who desired privacy. 'Will noon on Wednesday do?'

'I'll be there.'

Another surprise met Rane when she walked into the dining room and looked round for Leo. He was already waiting for her, unremarkable in a lounge suit, the blue velvet of the salon no longer in evidence. Marion was with him.

'You two met in Paris?' Rane nodded. She had met Marion twice, but she did not feel the need to tell Leo about the second encounter, and to her relief Marion, too, remained silent on the subject. Probably she had forgotten about it. The young mannequin had eyes only for Leo, and from the manner in which the latter met her shy glances, it was plain her feelings were reciprocated. A giddy sense of elation that had nothing to do with the wine sent Rane's winter blues flying.

'This is madness,' she scolded herself. 'All I know of the stranger is his Christian name.' Greville. It suited him, and haunted her. It touched her dreams at night with the same chaotic effect that his fingers had touched her arm. 'I don't even know his surname. Possibly I'll never set eyes on him again.' Her winter blues returned in full force. It was a probability, not a possibility, and she had to force her wandering mind to pay attention to what Leo was saying.

'The photographs of my Summer Collection for publication in *Dress*,' he launched into his topic with typical directness. 'I want them to be composite pictures, not just reproductions of individual garments. Oh, your photographs of the Spring Collection were absolutely fabulous. . . .'

'Thanks very much,' Rane replied drily, and Leo grinned.

'You don't need me to tell you your own strength in your profession,' he paid her the compliment of recognising her rightful place as one of the top ten photographers of the moment. 'But this time,' he went on enthusiastically, 'I want the photographs to show not only the clothes, but to suggest the whole way of life they're designed to grace.' He spread his hands in an expressive gesture. 'Elegant. Luxurious.'

'Wealthy?' Rane butted in quickly. They were back to their earlier conversation.

'Wealthy,' Leo replied promptly, and his chuckle told her he remembered.

'First find your background,' she challenged him.

'I already have.' He was one step ahead of her, and answered her enquiring look triumphantly. 'Fullcote Hall. It belongs to Marion's guardian, and it'd make an ideal background. It lies on the slopes of the Chiltern Hills.'

So did Whipsnade Zoo, Rane thought wryly, but it seemed a shame to tease the eager young Frenchman, so instead she said seriously,

'It's a departure, to show a collection at a venue other than Paris. Do you think it's a wise thing to do?' Leo had already shown a penchant for the unexpected, but was he making a mistake this time? she wondered. Dior might get away with it. But Leo? His first big showing received a rapturous reception, but success did not rest on the first rung of the ladder. Had he allowed his initial success to go to his head? Or, what was more likely, she deduced shrewdly, had he allowed his feelings for Marion to influence him unwisely? Until now Rane had respected the young designer's sound commercial judgment, but. . . .

'The actual showing won't be at Fullcote Hall.' This was a day of surprises, and Leo piled one on top of another until Rane began to lose count. 'The showing will be in Paris at the end of March as already arranged. I want the Collection photographed at

Fullcote Hall before that. Marion and I will be staying there for the first two or three weeks of March. . . .'

'We hoped you'd come and stay, too,' Marion burst in eagerly. 'Zilla and Shelley will be coming and going as they're needed for the pictures. They're the two older mannequins,' she elucidated, and Rane's depression deepened. Her work had brought her in contact with the two mannequins before. Zilla was about thirty, which made her Rane's senior by four years, and Shelley was her own age, and the teenager's unconsciously cruel description did nothing to lighten her spirits.

'You could call it a working house-party,' Leo grinned. 'But in between the photography sessions, you and Marion could relax and enjoy the countryside, while I work on the designs for my Autumn Collection.'

'But the first two or three weeks of March!' Rane expostulated. 'That's a month before the actual showing. Every day heightens the risk of someone getting to know the details of your Collection. What security arrangements have you made at Fullcote Hall?' They were back to their earlier conversation with a vengeance, and she pursued her theme with ruthless realism. 'You're taking an incredible risk,' she warned worriedly. 'After the massive response to your last Collection, one breath of what you're doing will bring newshounds with cameras homing in to the Chiltern Hills like bees round a honeypot, all intent on being the first to ferret out the secrets of your new season's designs. In case you're unaware of the impact you made on the fashion world, your last Collection was hot news,' she reminded him forcibly. 'One whisper that you've got your Collection finished so long before the showing, let alone intend to photograph it, is enough to make it a news item that you might find too hot to handle.

'We can cope,' Leo insisted. 'Fullcote Hall. . . .'

'Must have a staff to run it,' Rane interrupted him impatiently. 'Can you vouch for each and every one of them?'

'Oh, the staff at the Hall have all been with my guardian's family for centuries,' Marion exaggerated with an airy wave of her hand. 'They'd die rather than reveal a family secret.'

'What about Zilla and Shelley?' In her anxiety to push her point home, Rane excluded no one, not even the mannequins. 'A heavy bribe can be a big temptation, and there's such a thing as a long-range camera, if the person wielding it is told where to look for his picture. One whisper would be enough.' Although she did not know either of the two mannequins particularly well, it was common knowledge that Zilla enjoyed a lifestyle as exotic as her looks, a costly mode of living even on her high salary.

'Both the girls are top rank mannequins,' Leo argued. 'If the secrets of a Collection leaked before the showing, and even the slightest suspicion attached to them, their careers would be ruined, and they know it. They'd never get another assignment.'

'Which only leaves my guardian, and he wouldn't know a seam from a gather,' Marion grimaced. 'He disapproves of the whole fashion world on principle,' she laughed. 'Do say you'll come, Rane,' she begged earnestly. 'I'm sure you'll enjoy it much more than photographing Leo's Summer Collection amid the crush of a stuffy fashion salon.'

She would. And there was the added attraction that, at Fullcote Hall, there would be no danger of the stranger putting in an appearance. A change of scenery might even help to put him out of her mind.

'I'll come,' Rane accepted impulsively.

'Which only leaves us to drink to the success of the Summer Collection.' Leo raised his glass with a smile.

'*Only* to the success of the Collection?' Rane could not forbear to tease, as she allowed her glance to rest on the pair's linked hands, barely concealed beneath the tablecloth.

'It's a bit premature, to toast us.' To her surprise, the laughter vanished from the faces of her two companions, and they both looked glum.

'My guardian won't agree to us becoming engaged,' Marion explained miserably. 'Nothing I say can persuade him.'

'Go it alone,' Rane retorted robustly. 'You're over the age of consent.'

'I know I could, but I don't want to, it'd start our marriage off on the wrong footing if we had a family row beforehand,' Marion replied unhappily.

A guardian was hardly a family, but Rane felt it would be tactless to point it out in face of the girl's obvious depression, so she remained uneasily silent, and felt thankful when Leo jumped into the breach and saved her from having to reply.

'Marion's guardian seems to think all up-and-coming fashion designers are hopeless Bohemians,' he explained with a gloom equal to Marion's own. 'He thinks I'll drag Marion down to penury along with me. He disapproves of me as much as he disapproves of the fashion world I represent.'

'If you come to stay with us at the Hall, he might change his mind,' Marion urged. 'You're in the fashion world, too, even if it is a different branch of it, and no one could call you Bohemian. You're at the very top of your profession, secure, famous even.'

Rane felt anything but secure. This, then, was the

reason behind the invitation to stay at Fullcote Hall, not merely to photograph Leo's Summer Collection, but to act as an unwilling buffer between two young lovers and a stuffy, disapproving guardian. She viewed the prospect of her stay in the Chilterns with growing trepidation. Instead of being an antidote to her own problems, it bade fair to give her a lot of new ones, and now she had accepted, it was too late to back out.

High Wycombe gave her an early lunch, and some cheerful directions from a garage forecourt attendant who obligingly topped up her petrol tank.

'Fullcote Hall? You mean Mr York's place?'

'D'you know him?' It seemed silly to confess that she did not know the name of her host, only that he was Marion's guardian. By some discreet questioning, perhaps she could learn more about him, Rane thought hopefully. It was always useful to know the strength of the enemy.

'Not so you'd notice,' the attendant grinned. 'He keeps a low profile locally, does Mr York.'

'Ted, there's a customer here with a flat front offside!' The yell was impatient, and the attendant shrugged philosophically.

'Duty calls,' he grimaced.

'The directions,' Rane prompted him hastily before he could depart.

'Carry on along the A40 for a mile or two beyond West Wycombe, and then take to the lanes,' he advised. 'It's a pleasant run, and you'll find it well signposted.' His appreciative glance as he went into quick details pointed clearly enough to his admiration of Rane's slight figure, cosily clad against the biting wind in a full-length jade wool coat and matching skirt that enhanced the colour of her eyes, and a tan cashmere sweater which reflected the lights in her copper hair—suitable attire, she hoped, to allay the suspicions of a cantankerous guardian. She resisted an impish impulse to add pearls, and chose instead a chunky gold necklace and a matching bracelet to lighten the tailored severity of her outfit. They exchanged bright glints with the cheerful spring sunshine, that lost all illusion of warmth in competition with the cutting east wind that made her slide thankfully back into the driving seat and turn the bonnet in obedience with the attendant's directions.

Unlike many such, they proved remarkably accurate, and with the main road safely left behind her Rane relaxed and enjoyed the narrow lanes that dipped into picturesque villages, the flint cottages topped with weathered thatch, then rose again to reveal the lovely sweep of hills, hung with ancient stands of beech trees, bare still, like seal-brown sentinels waiting for the resurgence of new life to come, and the colourful glory that would be theirs at the crown of the year.

'Fullcote Hall, 2 miles.'

It boasted its own signpost. Rane's lips puckered into a moue. 'That could mean one of two things,' she muttered uneasily. Isolation, or importance. In the circumstances she relished the thought of neither. A disapproving guardian was bad enough, but a guardian who was also lord of the local manor, with feudal ideas about his own importance, was a good deal worse. Unconsciously her foot pressed down upon the brake pedal.

'Don't be a coward!' Almost aggressively Rane accelerated again, and within minutes sent the car skimming between high stone pillars on to a smooth wide tarmac driveway whose impeccable surface would have done credit to the motorway she had recently left. The drive led her through rich parkland, and finally curved round a broad shelter-belt of beech

trees to emerge with breathtaking suddenness in front
of Fullcote Hall itself.

'Leo was right. He was so right!' she breathed
ecstatically, and braked to a halt, absorbing the scene
presented to her.

Fullcote Hall lived up to its name. Murmurous
movement attracted her eyes to a large dovecote,
whose occupants, by their busy activity, clearly
delighted in the return of spring. Like a number of
cottages in the villages she had just passed through,
the cote was sturdily built of local flint, and
beautifully thatched, as was—Rane caught her breath
in delighted admiration—as was the Hall itself. The
house was low, and rambling, and gave the impression
that it had grown naturally from the ground on which
it stood, with its feet in a sea of waving daffodils that
rose from the surrounding lawns in yellow drifts, and
sent her one hand grasping for the handle of the car
door, and the other for her camera.

'Fullcote Hall isn't open to the public. The National
Trust property is further north from here.' The voice
was cold, forbidding, and oddly familiar. Rane spun
round.

'You!' she exclaimed in dismay.

He was taller, leaner, and even more devastatingly
handsome than she remembered. He was dressed
casually in a high-necked black sweater and black
slacks which accentuated his leanness and height, and
the labrador retriever at his heels, of the same Stygian
colour as his clothes, regarded her with a yellow stare
as unwelcoming as that of its master.

'What are you doing here?' She had no right to ask,
but her fast-hammering pulses panicked her into
asking just the same. Two weeks or more of trying to
change the mind of Marion's guardian was bad
enough, but with the stranger present as well to add to

her difficulties, her stay at Fullcote Hall would become impossible, Rane thought wildly.

'I've given the carriage a special polish for you, like you said, Mr York.'

'Thank you, Jack.' The stranger nodded to the man in groom's attire, and Rane felt a cold hand clutch at her stomach.

'Did he say, York?' she swallowed hard. 'Then you must be. . . .'

'The owner of Fullcote Hall,' he finished what her suddenly parched throat could not.

'And . . . and. . . .' She could not go on. She wished she had not bothered to put on her green coat and skirt; their tailored rightness in these surroundings would not impress this man. Nothing would, she realised despairingly. Fervently she wished she had not come.

'And Marion's guardian,' he confirmed, and his hard eyes told her several things besides the one unpalatable fact. They told her that he was fully aware of the reason why Marion had invited her to stay at his home. They told her that, as a champion of his ward's cause, she might just as well lay down her banner now, and go home, that whatever plans he might have for Marion's future were no concern of Rane's, and those plans would be brought to fruition in his own good time, no matter what she—or Marion, for that matter, Rane thought caustically—might decide to the contrary. And they told her, unmistakably, that Greville York would brook no interference from anyone, least of all from Rane, in the furtherance of those plans.

'I didn't know. . . .' She checked herself just in time. It was bad enough to face the possibility of the Paris stranger, and Marion's guardian, being two separate people. To discover them both rolled into one, and such a one, she thought shakily, was altogether too much. Her courage retreated in complete disarray, unhelped by her heart, which continued to behave in the same silly manner as it had done in the Paris fashion salon. With an immense effort that she felt uneasily certain must reveal itself in her expression, she marshalled the tattered remains of her self-control. She knew the strength of the enemy now, with a vengeance, she told herself unhappily, and had no hesitation in applying the appelation to Greville York. His grey eyes watched her, reading her confusion. Enjoying it, she told herself hardly, with a quick flash of temper that succeeded in steadying her as nothing else could have done. It was imperative that she did not reveal her weakness to her adversary. Their glances met and clashed, and the steel in his eyes left her in no doubt that he would take instant advantage of the slightest breach in her defences. It would be inviting disaster to lower her guard even for an instant, while she was in the company of this man.

'Rane! I'm so sorry, I didn't hear your car arrive.'

Marion came running towards them, looking like any leggy teenager in jeans and a chunky sweater, with her hair awry, and a tennis racquet in her hand. She paused and stooped to fondle the retriever.

'You should have come with me, Chip. You could have retrieved my balls for me. I was on the court at the back of the house,' she apologised. 'I didn't know you'd arrived until Jack, the groom, said he'd seen you with Greville. What a blessing you caught up with one another! I'd forgotten you'd met in Paris.'

It was far from a blessing that Greville had caught up with her. Rane winced at Marion's unfortunate choice of words, and wished heartily that she, too,

could forget the meeting in Paris. Forget Greville
York altogether. . . .

'If you spoil Chip's mouth with tennis balls, you'll
account to me, young lady,' Greville threatened
goodhumouredly. 'He's a gun-dog, trained to the field,
and his soft mouth is his most precious asset.' The
man's manner changed when he spoke to his ward,
and briefly Rane felt a flash of sympathy for his
attitude to Marion's proposed engagement. On her
knees on the gravel, with her tennis racquet flung
carelessly on the ground, and her arms round the
dog's neck impulsively hugging the animal to her,
Marion looked much younger than her eighteen years.
Younger, and very vulnerable. A tender girl on the
verge of womanhood, but who had not yet stepped
over the dividing line. A peach unripened, whose
tender bloom would bruise at the touch of a careless
hand. Unconsciously Rane glanced up at Greville, and
felt a sense of shock as she found her look returned
with one that probed her every thought, picking them
out of her mind to use against her. She caught her
breath, and her resolution hardened.

'Your ward's of age, it's up to her to choose.'
Courageously her eyes flashed a defiant message back
to him, ranging herself unequivocally on the side of
the young lovers. And against her host. Only the slight
narrowing of his grey stare told her that her message
had been received and understood. It gave her no
indication in return what moves he might make to
counter her championship, but she was unrepentant.
A peach could be bruised by too early picking, but it
could also wither if it was picked too late, or not at all.
Marion was young, and looked younger, but she was a
mannequin, already working at the hub of the world's
most competitive industry, and so could not be
completely naïve.

'Was Leo playing tennis with you?' Attack was the best form of defence, she decided spiritedly, and fired her first salvo by deliberately bringing Leo's name into the conversation.

'No, he. . . .'

'You must get Rane to give you a game,' Greville interrupted smoothly, ignoring Leo, and dodging her shots, Rane realised furiously, with humiliating ease. It was like firing at an invisible target, and she gritted her teeth in silence as he went on urbanely, 'The winter court's a hard one, and specially built so that it's sheltered from the wind. He paused, and then added deliberately, 'It makes a perfect trap for the sun on a day like this.'

Only for the sun? Rane's eyes flew to his face, trying to read his expression. If Greville disliked the thought of Marion's attachment to Leo so much, why had he allowed her to invite him to Fullcote Hall in the first place? He had opened his home not only to Leo, but to the paraphernalia of fashion advertising as well, so what ulterior motive had he got in mind? Rane eyed him suspiciously, but his face remained expressionless, and his level glance gave nothing away.

'I'm here to work, I shan't have time to play tennis,' she countered his suggestion repressively.

'You won't be working all the time.' It was a statement, not a question. An order, Rane realised angrily. The doves cooed, the sun shone, and the dog's tail made small thumping noises on the gravel as the animal responded to Marion's caress, and determination and defiance clashed like drawn swords across the idyllic scene.

'Come and see your room, Rane,' Marion interposed hastily. 'Jack will put your car away and bring your case up.'

'We'll meet again at dinner.' Greville clicked his fingers to his dog, divided a nod between the two girls, and strolled away, while Rane glared after his retreating back. Even if she was a guest in his house, he would not find her so obedient as his gun-dog, she vowed silently. 'We'll meet again at dinner.' Innocuous words, the pleasant comment of a genial host. To Rane they sounded like a challenge to a dual. She checked an impulse to bend and pick up a non-existent gauntlet.

'This room's nice, you'll have your own personal lullaby from the doves,' Marion drew her to the window to look out. 'The cote's built against this end of the house.'

The legendary gentleness of its occupants was the antithesis of the Hall's owner, Rane thought tartly. He was as hard as the flint from which the cote was built. And as unyielding. His manner towards Leo at dinner was outwardly impeccable. He included the younger man in the conversation with punctilious courtesy, and by the time she was halfway through her soup Rane began to relax. Before she had finished the hot, rich liquid, her throat became so tight with nervous tension that she could hardly swallow the last few spoonsful.

Greville talked easily, guiding the conversation as a good host should. Guiding it, Rane realised with wary alertness, to the constant disadvantage of the young designer. So this was to be Greville's tactics. Invite the opposition into your house, and fight him on home ground. Constantly show him at a disadvantage in front of Marion so that the girl could not hope to do other than contrast his shortcomings with her own luxurious background. As a strategy it was faultless. As behaviour towards a guest in his house, it was despicable, Rane told herself hotly.

'Your Palomino could do with some exercise, Marion. Jack's got his hands full at the moment with a mare in foal.'

Small talk—home talk. Where was it leading? Rane wondered tensely. She did not have to wait long to find out.

'Do you ride, d'Arvel?'

'Tell him, yes, Leo,' Rane begged silently. 'Tell him, yes, you're an expert horseman.'

'I've never had the opportunity, sir,' Leo fought back, and Rane wanted to cheer. She flashed a look of encouragement across the table to the young Frenchman.

'It serves Greville right,' she thought jubilantly. The 'sir' must have made her host feel as old as Methuselah.

'We've an old mare that's quiet, and completely trustworthy. The groom could ride with you, while Marion and I have a gallop.'

Underlining the delights Marion would forgo if she married Leo. Pointing out as clearly as a road sign that, if the girl attached herself to the young designer, she would be attaching herself to the equivalent of a ball and chain.

'I think perhaps it would be better if I remained behind. I have the sketches of my Autumn Collection to finish,' Leo countered.

It went on and on. Rane felt as if the sweet course would choke her. Before the dessert was finished she longed to cry, 'Stop it! Stop it, both of you!' and run from the room. She knew now how it felt to be a satellite in orbit, having radio waves bounced off it en route to another target. Each one left a sting that made eating impossible, and the strain was well nigh unbearable.

'Ladies?' The dinner was over at last, and Greville

glanced significantly at Marion.

'Don't be so formal, Greville, we're a family party, not a full-scale do!' To Rane's relief his ward thrust aside the implied suggestion that she and Marion should retire and leave the two men alone. Leo was battling back, but he was fighting a rearguard action, with the odds strongly against him, a boy against a man. The less time the two spent alone together, the better.

'Leo and I thought we'd go for a walk.' Rane's relief did not last long. 'Would you like to come with us, Rane?' Her expression said clearly that she did not expect Rane to accept the invitation. It was impossible to do so and play gooseberry, and yet it was equally impossible to refuse. To do so would mean being left alone with Greville, and the thought filled Rane with dread. Desperately she dredged up every woman's excuse for not doing what she did not want to.

'I think I'll go to bed early tonight,' she pleaded feebly. 'I've got a bit of a headache.'

'Perhaps a small brandy might help,' Greville suggested considerately, and handed one to her before Rane could refuse. 'Remember to be in by eleven,' he added as Marion and Leo took their departure. He directed his remark to his ward, but Rane did not doubt the warning was meant for her escort. It was insulting! He was treating the pair like irresponsible children, Rane fumed. It was a clever move, she acknowledged, more calculated to undermine than any amount of opposition, which at least had the merit of acting as a goad. To ignore their attachment, to refuse to treat the young pair seriously, was demoralising, and gave the victims nothing against which they could fight back.

'Does the curfew extend to me?' Rane spoke sharply into the silence, not giving Greville the opportunity to take charge of the conversation as the couple closed the doors behind them.

'Are you intending to go out again, before you finally go to bed?' He did not answer her question directly. He stoppered the brandy and strolled back to the fire with his own moderate goblet, but instead of sitting down he remained standing, leaning against the marble mantel, putting her at a disadvantage by making her look up at him from her low chair drawn up to the hearth. Using the same tactics with her as he had with Leo, she realised edgily.

'They won't work with me,' she fumed. Impulsively she jumped to her feet and answered him shortly. 'No, I intend to go to my room and sleep until morning. We've got a busy schedule ahead of us tomorrow, and I want to do as much as possible of the outdoor work while the sunshine holds.' Work that would effectively exclude her host, and legitimately keep Marion and Leo together for as much as she could possibly manage of the day, Rane planned vindictively.

'I need to go to my study, so I'll come with you as far as the stairs.'

Come with her, or escort her to make sure she went to her room as she declared she would, and did not slip out of doors without his knowledge? Rane's independent spirit rose. She was not accustomed to having to report her comings and goings to anyone, and she did not intend to start now with Greville York.

'I said I'd. . . .' she began indignantly, when her companion opened the double doors of the dining room and motioned her to precede him.

'Hmmm.' He paused and put a cautionary hand on her arm, drawing her back. Rane gasped at his touch as if she had been stung, and then went still, as she saw what had attracted his attention. Marion and Leo had not yet gained the front door. Oblivious to the world, they were locked in each other's arms, overlooked by an impassive suit of armour that, if it had a grain of sense—Rane criticised the ancient accoutrement of war unjustly—would have warned the young lovers so that they could escape before Greville espied them.

'I think perhaps we'd better wait a few minutes longer, don't you?' To Rane's amazement Greville quickly closed the two doors and regarded her with a look of quizzical amusement.

'Then you don't mind?' Sheer surprise shocked her into unguarded speech. 'But Marion said ... I thought. . . .' she stammered to a confused halt.

'What you saw is merely a manifestation of—what shall we call it? Spring fever?' Greville shrugged condescendingly. 'Like most of the malaises that afflict teenagers, it's best left to run its course.'

He made it sound as if the pair were no more than fourteen years of age, instead of respectively on each near side of twenty, and Rane's anger rose at his patronising manner.

'If it's spring fever, then be careful it isn't catching,' she taunted him recklessly.

She felt him go still. It was the stillness of a hovering eagle a second before it stoops, the breathless pause between lightning and thunder at the height of a storm. She gasped as the eagle stooped and the lightning struck, and the thunder was the hammering of her own pounding heart as Greville took her in his arms and drew her to him, and said in silky tones that held all the combined menace of the twin aerial threats,

'If it is, then we must both be infected, since we've both been in contact with them,' he said, and kissed her.

Not even a Frenchman could kiss like this. Rane's lips went numb under the aggressive pressure that scorned the fumbling efforts of an untried boy and plundered the soft fullness of her mouth with a deadly expertise that sent a shock wave of emotion through her like nothing she had ever experienced before. Her heart leapt wildly in her breast, and then went still, while her senses reeled with a sweet intoxication that had nothing to do with the brandy. In spite of herself her head tilted backwards, and her lips moved under his in an instinctive response.

'I must be mad. . . .' This was the man she had sworn to oppose, but he did not fight by the accepted rules. With unerring accuracy he pinpointed his adversary's weakness and exploited it to the full, and shame flooded Rane that she had allowed her weakness to become so easily apparent to him.

'Let me go!'

Desperately she fought to free herself from his hold, but she was caught in the encircling trap of his arms. Was this what he meant when, earlier, he used the word 'trap'? she wondered raggedly. She had been forewarned, so she should have been wary, but she had walked right into his trap and now it was too late. Despairingly she knew it would always be too late for her after this, that her heart would never be completely her own again. Terror gave her strength, and she hammered against his chest with small balled fists, pushed frantically against the steel-strong arms that encircled her, fighting to free herself. Fighting herself, she realised with a sob, as much as Greville.

'Let me go!' Her breath came in panting grasps, and with a final convulsive pull she tore herself free from his hold and fled from the room—from Greville; but she could not flee from herself.

The suit of armour marked her flight across the hall,

and watched with cold disdain as she stumbled up the wide stairway and out of sight into the blessed privacy of her room, where she slammed the door to behind her and flung herself shaking on the bed, knowing that all the doves in the cote could not coo a lullaby soothing enough to bring sleep to her tormented mind that night.

CHAPTER THREE

RANE deliberately left it as late as possible before she descended to breakfast the next morning. She took an unnecessary age donning her working gear of slacks and a thick sweater as a cover-up against the cold, and wished she could so easily cover up the ravages of the sleepless night that left her heavy-eyed and as disinclined for breakfast as she was to meet her host again. Would he triumph over his easy victory of the night before? Would he gloat, because he had succeeded in putting her to flight? Her heart hammered and she had to force her reluctant feet to descend the last of the stairs and cross the hall to the breakfast room door. She made a defiant face at the suit of armour as she turned the knob. Would he . . .?

He was not there. Except for Leo, and Zilla and Shelley who had travelled up from London that morning for the early modelling session, the breakfast room was empty. After nerving herself for the ordeal of meeting Greville again, Rane felt almost cheated that he was not there.

'Just coffee. Nothing to eat, thank you,' she refused the offer of the trim maid on duty at the laden sideboard.

'I don't see why you should bother to starve, you're not modelling.' The early start to the day did not appear to have improved Zilla's temper, and her tone was waspish.

'I'm not hungry,' Rane countered, and sat down beside Leo. She did not feel equal to a passage of arms with Zilla, and added quickly, before the latter could speak again, 'Where's Marion?' Greville's ward was not present either, and it was she who was due to work the first session.

'Out riding, with Greville,' Leo replied tersely, and Rane's sorely tried nerves gave way.

'How typical!' she exploded wrathfully. 'Greville knows full well we need Marion for the first session. I said last night at dinner that I wanted to get some shots of that blue dress against the background of the dovecote. The creeper-covered garden wall and the white doves, with the cote behind them, make a perfect foil for the cornflower blue silk, and the sun will only be in the right position for about an hour first thing in the morning. I suppose Greville thinks it's a clever move to take off with the one mannequin we need, just at the crucial moment, and put a spoke in the wheel of our work right from the start!'

'On the contrary, we went out early enough to enjoy our ride and be back in good time for breakfast, and for Marion to start work.'

His presence proved his point. Rane jumped violently as Greville spoke from just behind her, and scalding black coffee slopped over the rim of her cup and made a moat out of the saucer. Hastily she stood it on the table, hoping without conviction that Greville would not notice her agitation. He looked handsomer than ever in a perfectly fitting hacking jacket and breeches, and Rane's heart did a quick somersault as he helped himself from the sideboard and strolled towards the table. He dominated the room, and made everyone in it, herself included, Rane thought resentfully, seem like a mere satellite by comparison. Unconsciously she held her breath as he paused before selecting a chair, then let it out in a puff of what she staunchly told herself was relief, when he drew out a seat beside Zilla and Shelley, and proceeded to exchange pleasantries with the two mannequins. Zilla's black eyes slid across the table in a quick look of triumph, and depression descended upon Rane as Marion brought her choice from the sideboard to eat beside her.

'Porridge?' she teased, making an effort to shake herself out of her dark mood.

'You'll put on inches.' Zilla's tone was barbed.

'I can eat what I like, it doesn't affect my weight,' Marion laughed, and the older mannequin scowled. Her high-cheekboned face lost its classic beauty when she scowled, Rane noted dispassionately. The pitiless early morning sunshine gave it a haggard look that spoke volumes for the stringent dieting Zilla found necessary in order to keep her figure.

'Make the most of it. In a few years' time it'll be a different story.' Shelley spoke without rancour, and Rane felt a flash of thankfulness for her easygoing nature, which she found much easier to work with than Zilla's sharp spite.

'Before that time comes, Marion can give up modelling, she doesn't need to work.' Greville spoke to Shelley, but his target had got to be Leo. Rane caught her breath, and her glance swivelled between the two.

'What a start to the morning!' she thought edgily. It was bad enough having to deal with a temperamental mannequin and a highly strung designer, increasingly nervous during the run-up to the showing of his next Collection, without having to run the gauntlet of the tense undercurrents that made the atmosphere in the breakfast room positively electric. Rane felt as if, at any moment, the air might begin to crackle. Marion looked miserable, and Leo sulky, while Zilla—Rane slanted the older mannequin a glance of pure dislike— Zilla looked as if she was thoroughly enjoying herself, sitting on the sidelines and watching the upset she had helped to create. Only Shelley seemed unaffected. Her ash-blonde hair and brown eyes were as striking a contrast to Zilla's sultry darkness as the difference in their natures, and Rane regretted that Shelley was not taking a larger share in the photography sessions.

'Time to go.' Leo jumped to his feet, his expression tense.

'Don't leave your sketches behind,' Rane warned him, indicating the portfolio through which his restless pencil worked even while he ate his breakfast.

'I'll take them up to Marie. I'm going to get changed,' Marion offered obligingly.

'Tell her to put them under lock and key,' Leo said curtly, and handed the portfolio to Marion to give to the elderly dresser, who now reigned supreme in an upstairs room along with the precious Summer Collection about to be photographed. The girl quit the room with the sketches, and Rane held her breath. The portfolio contained the nucleus of Leo's Autumn Collection, and she knew, none better, the need to keep its contents absolutely secret. Nevertheless, deliberate, or simply ill-considered, Leo's remark could be construed as an insult to his host.

'I'll come with you, Leo. I want to discuss angles,' Rane said hastily. She did not. She had already decided from which angles she intended to take her morning's photographs, but she wanted, most urgently, to remove Leo from Greville's vicinity before the young Frenchman was provoked into an open clash with his host. Bitterly she blamed Greville for driving him to the brink. If trouble flared between the two, she had no doubt Leo would be the loser, and this in turn would react on Marion, and. . . .

'Come *on!*' Urgently she grabbed Leo's hand, and pulled him with her towards the door.

'I'll follow Marion, and get changed myself.' Shelley rose and came after them. 'Coming, Zilla?' she enquired over her shoulder.

'What, go out in this freezing wind until I absolutely have to? Certainly not,' Zilla refused promptly. 'I'll stay here with Greville, and wait until I'm wanted,' she purred, looking, Rane thought vindictively, like a cat that has unexpectedly come across a bowl of cream.

'I'll come out later and watch the proceedings,' Greville promised, and Rane's heart sank. It sounded more like a threat than a promise, and with tension already running high, Greville's presence at the modelling session could only make things worse. Perhaps that was what he intended? Rane's stomach curled into a tight knot at the prospect of him looking on while she took photographs, watching her every move, doubtless criticising. If she felt on edge, how much worse must Leo feel at the prospect?

'Lift your foot a little higher. The skirt must fall—so.' Leo bent and patiently adjusted the drape of the skirt for the umpteenth time, and Rane longed to shout at him.

'Hurry, Leo! Hurry and get it over before Greville comes out.' She gripped her fingers tightly together in the wide sleeves of her duffle coat, and trying in vain to still their trembling that would surely produce camera shake, and ruin all her photographs unless she could bring it under better control.

'The creeper's sticking in my leg,' Marion wailed. 'This wall's about the most uncomfortable place on earth to sit on!'

'Never mind your leg,' the designer retorted callously. 'The dress must look absolutely right.' Leo was a perfectionist, and neither the biting wind nor hostility from Marion's guardian could dissuade him from his high standards. The cornflower blue wild silk, with its bloused bodice and tightly belted waist, was every girl's desire, and Marion was the ideal mannequin to model the delicate summer dress, Rane acknowledged. She had the youthful looks, the fresh attractiveness that the dress demanded, and there was no doubt Leo had had it made to measure for her. Rane wondered idly if he intended to give it to her as a present after the showing at the end of the month.

'If you spend another second fussing about with that hemline, I'll freeze to death perched on top of this wall,' Marion grumbled. 'My bottom's already numb from sitting on the stone.'

'Your derrière will come to no harm for the sake of another minute or two.'

Nerves were frayed, and no doubt tempers would shortly follow. Rane sighed philosophically, and thanked her lucky stars she was not a mannequin. The glamour of the profession was only on the surface, she decided, watching the two at work. Modelling winter clothes in the middle of a heatwave, and flimsy summer dresses, as now, in the teeth of a biting March wind, while still managing to look serene and perfectly groomed, was only a part of the long hours of arduous work, and sometimes downright privation, as instanced by the unnatural slenderness of Zilla's tall figure, that ensured the mannequins earned every penny of their high fees.

'Hasn't Greville come out yet?' Shelley joined her, enveloped from head to foot in a voluminous cloak that effectively covered every inch of the dress she herself was modelling, a sign that Leo was cognisant of the risk he took in exposing his Collection so long before the actual showing.

'No, he's still in the house with Zilla,' Rane replied shortly, and felt grateful that the deep hood of her duffle coat hid her expression from her companion.

'Lucky Zilla,' Shelley grinned. 'Rich men, and those who're young and handsome, don't usually come wrapped in the same package, and one who's loaded with diamonds to boot. . . .' She gave an expressive whistle.

'Diamonds?' The allusion escaped Rane. She was not particularly interested, but anything was better, even talking about Greville, than trying to escape the image of his lean face, which persisted in intruding between herself and her concentration on the work in hand.

'Didn't you know?' Shelley asked, surprised. 'Greville's the York in York & Steele, the Hatton Garden diamond merchants. Marion's father was the Steele.'

'Was?' Rane gave herself a mental shake. She was talking in monosyllables. She was thinking in much the same way, except that it was two syllables, not one, which hammered unceasingly through her weary mind, driving every other thought into the background. Greville . . . Greville . . . Greville. . . .

'Marion's parents were killed in a plane crash about four years ago. She'd got no other relatives, so Greville took on the responsibility of being her guardian.'

'That explains why he's so concerned about who Marion marries,' Rane spoke half to herself. 'The diamonds, I mean.'

'You mean fortune-hunters,' Shelley put it more bluntly.

'I'm sure Leo's not a fortune-hunter,' Rane vigorously championed the young designer. 'And anyway, nothing can excuse the way Greville treats him. He is, after all, a guest at Fullcote Hall.'

'I wouldn't know about that, since I'm not staying here,' Shelley shrugged. 'But if Greville's so concerned about Marion picking up the wrong beau, why doesn't he marry her himself?' she asked practically. 'There can't be such a huge disparity in their ages, and twelve or so years isn't unusual when the seniority is on the man's side. It'd be the ideal solution.'

The ideal solution for whom? Rane winced away from the suggestion. Not for Marion, certainly, who had eyes only for Leo. Not for Zilla, she thought wryly, who had both eyes firmly fixed on Greville, or what was more likely, on Greville's diamonds. And least of all for herself, she acknowledged unhappily, caught inescapably in the trap of a hatchet-cut, rock-jawed face, and a pair of clear grey eyes.

'*Voilà!*' Leo rose to his feet and stood back to survey his handiwork. 'Don't move an inch, Marion,' he warned.

'I couldn't if I wanted to, I'm frozen into a solid block of ice,' she grumbled feelingly.

'I'll be as quick as I can,' Rane promised sympathetically, and thrust back the hood of her duffle coat the better to see what she was doing. The wind ran frozen fingers through her hair, ruffling it into a halo about her heart-shaped face. It bit at her finger ends and helped to steady their trembling as she adjusted her camera and put her eye experimentally to the view-finder.

'Half a dozen shots should be enough.' The white straw hat with the cornflowers decorating the brim, thrown carelessly at Marion's feet; the half a dozen white moon-daisies dangling from her fingers; even the sun, were all in exactly the right position for the perfect picture. The grey-brown flint of the dovecote made an ideal foil in the background. Only the doves were missing.

'I simply *must* have them in the picture.' Rane tilted her camera this way and that to get them into range, but her efforts merely succeeded in blotting out the dress, while the doves, stubbornly refusing to co-operate, continued to strut and preen maddeningly on the very top of the cote, out of range.

'It's because we're all milling around down here, I expect. It's frightened them off.'

'Let's go away, and perhaps they'll come down again.'

On a warm day it might have been a good idea. 'I'm not going to sit here indefinitely, waiting for doves to ground,' Marion mutinied. 'I'll die of pneumonia before you get your first shot!'

'You need corn,' Greville declared confidently, and Rane's head jerked round. Her fingers closed convulsively about her camera, and the shutter clicked before she could prevent it.

'There, now you've made me waste my film!' She turned on Greville angrily. 'I've got a perfect picture of your gravel drive!' she stormed, blaming him for the waste, for the fright he had given her by coming up behind her unawares, for her madly thumping heart that brought the palsy back to her unnerved fingers. The gravel should have crunched beneath his feet, and warned her of his approach. She blamed the inoffensive gravel chippings as well, as she fought to regain her self-control. 'We need the doves,' she snapped, and tried unsuccessfully to make herself believe that they were all that was needed. Marion looked as if she needed a mustard bath to thaw her out. Leo's expression said clearly that Greville's presence was the last thing *he* needed.

'But I need Greville,' her heart mourned. 'I'll never cease to need him.' Every nerve of her ached for him with a longing that threatened to consume her.

'Stand still for a moment, everybody.' To her chagrin Greville took control of the session easily, naturally, ignoring the seething resentment on the young Frenchman's face, as with a confident hand he dug into his pocket and brought it out filled with wheat seed, which he proceeded to scatter with a graceful movement that reminded Rane irresistibly of an old-fashioned sower, while at the same time he whistled softly through his teeth in a low, coaxing call that was curiously attractive.

The doves came. She should have known they would, for Greville. One by one they fluttered down, until soon a murmuring flock was settled busily at the foot of the wall.

'Is that where you want them?'

She had not told him where in the picture she needed the doves. Perversely Rane wished the birds had alighted anywhere but within camera range, but with unerring accuracy Greville drew them to the very spot where they would make her picture complete.

'Take your shots quickly, Rane, and let me get off this wall and back to somewhere warm,' Marion begged pitifully.

'Take my cloak.' Shelley generously took off her own warm covering as Marion at last descended stiffly from her seat on the cold stone the moment Rane gave her the signal that she had taken enough shots.

'Oh, you've made the doves fly!' Impulsively Shelley lifted her arms towards the affrighted flock. 'Take another shot, Rane, quick!'

Instinctively Rane obeyed him. The urgency of Greville's tone impelled her eye to the view-finder, and her finger to the shutter. The picture was a poem in white. The mannequin's ash-blonde hair and the crisply pleated skirt of her white cotton dress were lifted high by the strong breeze, her arms lifted to the cloud of fluttering white wings. Afterwards, Rane took more shots of Shelley in the white dress, against different backgrounds, but she knew there would not be another to equal the one Greville had ordered her to take, and the certainty acted as a rasp on her professional pride. Almost she wished she had disobeyed him, and risked losing the shot. Almost. . . .

'That's the lot.' She came to the end of her film. There would have been one more shot left if Greville had not startled her into pressing the shutter and taking a picture of the gravel drive. Crossly she tried to think of another shot she might have taken to equal the one with the flying doves, if only she had had the capacity for one more, but try as she might it eluded her, and her failure served only to increase her irritation.

'As soon as Zilla's done her stint, we must be off back to London.' Shelley hurried with them towards the welcome shelter of the house.

'I shan't be ready for Zilla until late this afternoon,' Leo said emphatically. 'I want first to attend to the hemline on the blue silk. I'm not satisfied that it looks just right.'

'But, Leo. . . .'

But Leo was already hurrying Marion upstairs to Marie, the elderly dresser, where doubtless he would spend the next few hours agonising over the hemline of the cornflower blue silk.

'I must be back in town by mid-afternoon.' Shelley looked concerned. 'I've got another assignment at four o'clock.' She was a freelance, so her time was precious, and she as well as Rane had expected to get most of the work done by lunchtime. 'I begged a lift in Zilla's car this morning, my own's in for service, and if I have to wait until Leo's finished with her. . . .'

'I'll run you to the nearest railway station,' Rane offered quickly. 'In fact, you can take my film in to the office for me, if you will.' The contents made it imperative that the film be delivered by hand, and Shelley was a completely trustworthy courier. 'If you drive the car in to the station, I'll write a note to Clive on the way.' With Leo and Marion ensconced with Marie, and Shelley gone, she would be left with the unenviable choice of either Zilla or Greville for company, and Rane congratulated herself on the neatness with which she had managed to dodge them both.

'I don't know about driving your car, Rane,' Shelley looked doubtful. 'I've never handled an automatic before.'

'I'll take you both in my car,' Greville settled the matter firmly.

'If you take Shelley to the station, there's no need for me to come as well,' Rane promptly sidestepped his offer.

'You wanted to write your note on the way,' Greville countered, and overruled her even as she opened her lips to argue. 'There's no time for you to do it before we set off, if Shelley's to catch the lunchtime train back to town.'

Once again Rane was caught in a trap of his setting. Frustration and resentment raised her temperature sufficiently for her to ignore the keen bite of the wind, and she rounded on him angrily as Shelley fled indoors to change.

'I suppose I'm allowed time to go and collect some notepaper from my room?' she asked sarcastically.

'There's no need,' Greville replied, 'you'll find all that's necessary is already in the car.'

The notepaper was thick and cream-coloured, with matching lined envelopes neatly housed in a pull-out that did duty as a writing desk immediately behind the chauffeur's seat in the long grey Bentley, a facility that spoke of industrious hours during the journeys undertaken by the sleek car's owner.

The chauffeur was not in evidence. Greville took the wheel himself, and Shelley sat beside him, and Rane did not know whether to feel left out or reprieved, sitting in the back by herself. The reprieve would not be for long. 'So make the most of it,' she warned herself, and applied her energy to writing a short explanatory note to Clive to go with the film, trying not to think of the journey back, alone in the car with Greville.

'I'll see Clive gets your packet safely, Rane. 'Bye!'

The train disappeared Londonwards, carrying Shelley along with it, and Greville said.

'You look cold. Let's have a coffee before we start back.'

'The station buffet's nearest.' Rane refused to be humiliated by appearing in her working gear in the kind of hotel lounge Greville would doubtless frequent.

'Two coffees, please.' To her surprise Greville made no demur, and drank the steaming beverage with every evidence of enjoyment. He seemed to see no incongruity in drinking his elevenses from a plastic beaker on a windy station platform, while his Bentley waited for him at the entrance. Rane eyed the car curiously as they returned.

'What are you looking at?' Greville enquired interestedly, and she flashed him an amused glance.

'Your number plates,' she confessed. 'I thought on a car like this you might have personalised plates. GY 1 or something like that.' It would be appropriate to complement his style of living, she thought.

'I don't carry an identity badge to advertise my presence.' Greville opened the front passenger door for her, and waited until she was comfortably settled inside. 'So far as is possible in a car of this calibre, I prefer to travel incognito.' He keyed the engine into life and added casually, 'On occasions I've even been known to travel by bus.'

Curiously, Rane believed him. In spite of his wealth, and the power it must give him, he seemed to have little personal vanity. She stole a glance at his face, and the garage man's comment returned to tease her.

'He keeps a low profile locally, does Mr York.'

His profile was clean cut, and heart-stoppingly handsome, and a lot more photogenic than all three of the mannequins rolled into one.

'I don't keep a personalised number-plate on my person, either.' He turned his head and grinned at her, and Rane's cheeks warmed.

'The need for secrecy is just as important in the fashion business as it is in the diamond trade,' she retaliated sharply. He had sensed her eyes upon him, probably guessed at her thoughts, and was openly laughing at her for them. She hated him for laughing at her.

'You can hardly compare the two.' He turned the big car into a roadside layby fronting a panoramic view of the hills that Rane felt too angry to appreciate properly. He braked, then leaned back in his seat and cut the engine, surveying her aloofly from several inches above her head. 'The fashion world's nothing but a butterfly existence, here today and gone tomorrow,' he pronounced. 'There's no future in fashion. Diamonds are different. Diamonds are for ever.' His tone, his look, were as hard as his diamonds, Rane thought cuttingly. Clearly he was referring to Leo's prospects, as well as to the fashion world in general, and her hackles rose in defence of what was her own world as well.

'Don't be so superior,' she snapped. 'Of course there's a future in fashion. There'll always be a future in clothes, unless the human race reverts to wearing woad,' she flashed cuttingly. 'Leo's designs *are* the future,' she insisted, courageously bringing names and personalities into the arena. 'Leo's a pacer in the fashion world, out in front by a head.'

'Pacers are only put into a race to allow the favourite a quick sprint to the winning post at the end,' Greville reminded her harshly.

Checkmate. Once again he exposed the weakness in her argument, and frustration at his easy mastery roused Rane's temper to boiling point and made her throw caution to the winds.

'If you don't care for the analogy, then I'll put it another way,' she cried, thoroughly roused by now, and careless of the consequences. 'You say diamonds are for ever. So are fashionable clothes. And so is love!' She flung the word at him like an arrow, seeking to pierce his impenetrable armour. Seeking to wound.

'Love?' He did not pretend to misunderstand her. His eyes narrowed, hardened, and his voice cut like a whip. 'What does Marion know of love? She's a teenager, not long out of finishing school. Her attraction to this Frenchman is nothing but infatuation. She's not experienced enough to know the difference.'

'Are you?'

It was said. A split, fear-filled second later, Rane wished it unsaid, but it was that infinitesimal moment of time too late. The closed car door barred her way of escape. Frantically she pressed herself back against the luxurious hide upholstery, cringing to evade his reaching hands, but they closed about her upper arms, drawing her towards him effortlessly as if her weight was no more than that of a child, until she rested, half sitting, half lying across his lap, her head pressed back across the crook of his arm, and her face upturned to his, at the mercy of his descending lips.

'Are you?' He taunted her with her own words, and the hard line of his face mocked her inability to answer him as he stopped her feeble attempt to speak with the crushing pressure of his mouth upon her own. It managed only a small, inarticulate sound as she struggled to sit up, but his arms held her as if in a vice, while his kiss changed and deepened, moving provocatively across her mouth, seeking, exploring, demanding an answer that she dared not give even if she could.

Rane closed her eyes lest he should read the answer in their stricken depths, and instantly his lips sealed her lids so that, bereft of sight, her other senses became more urgently, vitally alive, responding to his virile strength that strained her close, and closer.

'Greville. . . .' It was a whisper. A whimper. A submission. Her arms reached up to clasp themselves round his neck, her fingers played in the crisp, smooth darkness of his hair, and her lips parted, beseeching him to close them with his own. If she had not done so before, for good or ill Rane knew the difference now, even if Marion did not.

CHAPTER FOUR

'Do you?'

Greville altered the wording, but the question was the same. And so was the mockery, Rane saw furiously. He straightened up and leaned back easily in his seat, looking down at her white face with a light in his eyes that suggested the verge of laughter.

'Let me up!' A wave of scarlet drove away the whiteness, and Rane fought her way to a sitting position on his lap.

'Hey, mind where you're digging your elbows!'

'It's your own fault if you're in their way!' She used them without mercy as she struggled to slide herself off his lap and regain her seat on the passenger side of the car. After what seemed an age she felt the hard muscular legs under her give way to smooth hide upholstery, and she raised trembling hands to straighten her tumbled curls. A sob rose in her throat, and she choked it down.

'I hate you!' His kisses were a mockery, torn from her lips to satisfy his own ego. She felt cheated, humiliated, used—and angrier than she had ever been in her life before. Her heart wept that his kisses were not for real, not for her, but only as a tool to serve his mockery, but ruthlessly she silenced its mourning and shouted at him to drown its crying voice.

'Find someone else to amuse yourself with! Try Zilla,' she spat vindictively. 'She might appreciate your attentions, I don't,' she lied valiently.

'I might do just that,' Greville retorted savagely, with a mercurial change of mood that drove his hand

to key the engine into life, while his other wrenched at
the steering wheel in a vicious turn that whitened his
knuckles on the rim and raised on anguished screech
from the tyres as the big car leapt into motion like a
cruelly rowelled horse, driving Rane back into her seat
with the sudden forward thrust of it. The countryside
rushed towards them through the wide screen, and she
knew swift fear as her eyes registered the soaring
speedometer needle. Fifty—sixty—seventy. She longed
to cry out to him to slow down. And then she just
longed to cry. She stole a glance at his set face beside
her, and the sharp edges of his profile blurred with the
realisation that he would not notice if she watched him
openly. His hands on the wheel were relaxed, his
knuckles no longer showing white, his touch feather-
light on the powered steering, in perfect control of the
fast speeding machine, and the tense, charged
moments behind them put on one side as if they had
never occurred. Rane envied him and loathed him for
his ability to so easily put them aside, moments that
burned an indelible mark on her own heart as his
kisses burned her still throbbing lips.

'Zilla's waiting for you,' she pointed out maliciously,
breaking the tense silence between them as the Bentley
rolled to a halt at the front entrance to Fullcote Hall.
Independently she turned her back on Greville and
reached for the handle of the car door.

'It's locked!' she discovered furiously. Perhaps she
was pulling the wrong handle? The Bentley was as far
removed from her own small runabout as the Q.E.2
from a rowing boat, and its accessories were strange to
her. Hastily she tried another handle with similar
results, and her temper snapped. 'If you're trying to
be funny. . . .' She rounded on Greville angrily.

'The doors are locked electrically,' he informed her
curtly. 'If you'll have the patience to wait for a second

or two, I'll open it for you.' His hand, and the handle under her fingers, moved almost in unison. The door beside her opened smoothly and caught her unawares. Her fingers still clung to the handle, and the coach-built weight of the upholstered door swung open and carried her along with it.

'Loose the door. . . .'

Greville was a second too late. Unprepared for its swing, Rane went along with it, and ejected on to the gravel drive in an undignified scramble that succeeded in saving her balance, but not her pride.

'So that's where you went! Leo's been looking everywhere for you.'

Why did it have to be Zilla waiting on the steps to witness her humiliation? Zilla, who had sworn not to come outside in the wind until it was absolutely necessary, but braved it cheerfully enough in order to greet Greville's return. It was obvious from her expression that she had not expected to greet Rane as well. She scrambled to her feet, her face scarlet with mortification. No doubt Zilla will put the wrong construction on my blushes as well, she thought furiously.

'Leo knew I was taking Shelley to the station,' she snapped unguardedly. She had not taken Shelley to the station. Greville had, and she had gone along with him for the ride, and it was plain that Zilla was furious about it, and the blaze in her black eyes warned Rane that the other girl would not easily forgive her for trespassing on what she obviously considered to be her own special preserve.

'If you'd been here when you were wanted, I could have got my modelling session over and taken Shelley back to town myself.'

'Leo said he wouldn't be ready for you until late this afternoon.'

It was degenerating into an undignified squabble. Not for the first time, Rane wished she was several inches taller. The models were all of queenly height, if not, in Zilla's case, of queenly disposition, and retaliation lost its impact when you had to look up at someone to deliver it. It annoyed Rane even more that she had to look up a further several inches to Greville's six feet plus. Beside him Zilla had the advantage of her, and knew it. Together they made an ideally matched pair.

'Do say you'll come and watch my boring old modelling session this afternoon!' Zilla slipped her hand through Greville's arm as if she had known him all her life, and flashed him a brilliant smile as she turned and walked with him up the steps to the house.

'I wouldn't miss it for the world,' Greville assured her gallantly. 'What background have you chosen for the clothes you're modelling?'

This from the man who professed to despise the fashion world! Rane felt slightly sick. A pretty face, a fawning manner, and flatter their vanity, and any woman could twist a man round her little finger, she told herself disgustedly. Any woman, she amended bleakly, except herself.

'Leo mentioned the lake and the swans as a background,' Rane butted in determinedly, refusing to be discounted. Zilla did not choose the background any more than she chose which clothes she had to model.

'Swans are hardly my scene.' Zilla turned a sultry look on Greville. 'I'm modelling going-away clothes. Travelling clothes.' She cast a suggestive look at the parked Bentley, and Rane's eyebrows rose. Surely Greville wouldn't . . .?

'Use the Bentley by all means,' he offered with an indulgent smile, and her eyebrows rose even further.

'Or better still,' he capped his generosity, 'use my private jet as a background, it would complement your travelling outfit.' He made it sound as if it would complement Zilla rather than her travelling outfit, and Rane's lip curled. Greville, for all his wealth and power, was no better than any man, and Rane did not need to look at Zilla's face to see the triumph reflected there. 'So long as the number plate and identification marks don't show on the photographs, I've no objection to you using both.' He spoke authoritatively to Rane, and she bridled at his tone, that instructed her as if she was a mere appendage to the mannequin, she thought furiously.

'Leo might not want either of them as a background,' she retorted sharply, and wished uncharitably that Leo might refuse the offer. She wished in vain, and looked on in silent chagrin as the designer enthusiastically fell in with the suggestion, apparently not willing to allow his private feelings to stand in the way of any offer that would project the image he desired for his precious Summer Collection.

The rest of the day, indisputably, belonged to Zilla, and the mannequin made the most of every minute. Like Leo, Rane was forced to subjugate her feelings to the job in hand. It was not easy, and Zilla went out of her way to make it even more difficult. She moved, deliberately, Rane felt angrily certain, just as Rane was about to press the shutter, which necessitated several shots having to be taken again. She fidgeted and fussed to a degree that put Leo's fussing in the shade, and between the two Rane was hard pressed to restrain her temper.

She took shots of Zilla posing beside the plane, its sleek silver lines a perfect foil for the scarlet and white patterned silk duster coat with the flyaway back, covering a white crêpe dress with knife-edge pleats that emphasised the excessive slenderness of the mannequin's figure as they flowed vertically from a high bodice through a narrow belt of the same bright scarlet as the coat.

She photographed Zilla stepping from the wide open door of the Bentley, dressed in a black sheath cocktail dress that looked as if it had been poured over her perfect contours. No one looking at the subsequent photograph could guess at the large bulldog clips that gripped the surplus material at the back, Rane's emergency standby for a garment being modelled by a mannequin whom it was not designed to fit.

Zilla paraded draped chiffon, and rich ivory shantung, in their turn up the steps of the old house. She leaned languidly against one of the tall columns beside the impressive doorway to the Hall, to show off a fine wool suit of pearl grey, with a wide collar and tightly belted waist, set off with an array of heavy jet beads that only Zilla could wear with aplomb.

Chic clothes. Exotic clothes. Garments in which every woman should look her best, and Zilla did, and knew it. She posed and preened, looked haughty as only classic beauty can, then melted into smiles for Greville's benefit.

'Playing to the gallery,' Rane muttered scornfully.

'Did you say something?'

'No,' she denied crossly. She had not realised Greville was close enough to her to hear. She wished he would go away. She felt scruffy, grubby, and untidy in her working gear, beside Zilla's glossy perfection, and Greville would be less than human if he did not compare the two, to her own disadvantage. The knees of her slacks were dusty from contact with the gravel drive as she knelt to obtain an upwards angle on one of the shots. The toes of her shoes were scuffed by the same abrasive agent, and her temper felt as ill-used as both.

'That's enough. Let's call it a day.' Leo declared himself satisfied at last.

'Not before it's time,' Rane muttered ungraciously, and snapped her camera shut with a force that did more to relieve her feelings than it did to help her camera.

'Bother!' she exploded wrathfully.

'What's the matter?' Greville bent an interested eye as she struggled with the mechanism.

'I've bent the fastener, and it's jammed inside. This is *all* I need!' She surveyed her hapless instrument with mounting dismay.

'You should treat delicate mechanism with more care,' Greville pontificated, and Rane drew in a quivering breath. At that precise moment she would dearly have loved to bend the delicate mechanism further still, across his dark, uncaring head. With an immense effort she restrained the impulse, and he went on, unaware of his narrow escape. 'There's an excellent camera shop a few yards from the station, just beyond where we parked this morning. There's still time to get it mended before they close.'

'I'll find it for myself,' Rane refused shortly before he had time to offer to take her there.

'I was going to suggest,' he spoke evenly, 'that as you'll be *driving yourself* there,' the steely emphasis he put on the words penetrated like a knife, and angry red suffused Rane's cheeks, 'as you'll be *driving yourself* there, you'd do better to remain on the main road, rather than take the more scenic route we drove along this morning.' He clearly had no intention of offering to drive her there himself, and Rane should have felt glad, but instead she felt angrier than ever, mostly with herself for the sick disappointment that assailed her.

'I suppose I must be on my way, as well.' Zilla was

patently reluctant. 'I do so dislike driving in the dark,' she hinted.

'If you start now, you'll be back in town long before it even gets dusk,' Rane butted in impatiently, venting her anger on the mannequin, and repaying her for the latter's temperamental behaviour during the afternoon.

By the time she reached the camera shop, she had the grace to feel ashamed of her outburst. The solitary drive calmed her nerves, and she emerged with her camera and her temper once more intact, and impulsively turned her car to follow the same return route she and Greville had taken that morning. It wound in and out among the lanes, and she had some difficulty in finding her way, but by dint of map reading and perseverance she at last managed to strike the right road.

'He shan't dictate to me which road I must take,' she muttered rebelliously, unwilling to acknowledge, even to herself, that it was something that went deeper than mere rebellion which beckoned her compulsively along the route she and Greville had travelled together, and made her turn her wheels and park on the same pull-in, staring through her own much smaller windscreen at the superb view, that was totally obscured by the tears she was too proud to let fall. They prevented her from noticing another car draw in behind her until a voice hailed her through her open window.

'It's Rane Strickland, of *Dress*, isn't it? I thought I couldn't be mistaken!'

Rane blinked the newcomer's face into focus, and immediately went tense.

'What are you doing in this part of the world?' he asked her chattily.

'I'm on holiday,' she lied. Quickly she pulled herself

together. 'What about you?' she enquired suspiciously. There could only be one reason for Gus Crawford of the *Echo* to leave his usual haunts among the bars and bright lights of the metropolis, and that was because he scented a story, and among the sleepy villages and distant vistas surrounding Fullcote Hall there could only be one story that would interest a newspaper reporter from the popular press, and that was Leo's Summer Collection. All Rane's previous misgivings rose in a rush to confront her.

'I warned Leo,' she breathed worriedly. 'Why didn't he listen? Why didn't I try harder to dissuade him?' She could have refused to come to Fullcote Hall to photograph his Collection. Consent was tacit agreement with his madcap scheme, and she blamed herself bitterly for encouraging the young designer.

'Would you believe, I'm on holiday, too?' She did not believe him. Just as, obviously, he did not believe her, she realised with dismay, and lied again when he persisted,

'Whereabouts are you staying?'

'I'm touring. Just passing through.' The lack of welcome in her tone hoped the same applied to him, and he grinned at her, unabashed by her distant manner.

'See you around, then.'

'Not if I can help it,' Rane muttered to herself fiercely, and watched through her driving mirror as he jack-knifed himself back behind the wheel of a battered sports car, waving blithely as he roared away along the road. Rane did not return the wave. She sat gnawing her lip, and watching the retreating car with anxious eyes.

'He didn't believe me when I said I was just passing through,' she worried. 'Ten to one he'll wait somewhere in a side turning off the road, and follow me, just to make sure.' She had experienced the reporter's tactics before, and did not like them or him. 'I'll have to put him off the scent somehow, I daren't let him follow me to Fullcote Hall.'

The next turn of the road brought a sizeable hostelry into view, and a ready solution to her problem. Its creaking sign, The Wheelback, proclaimed the chair-making industry for which the district was famed, and hospitably offered its car park for her to pull on to.

'I'll walk straight in as if I'm a resident,' she planned gleefully. It was too early for the public rooms to be open, so if the reporter was watching he could only draw one conclusion from her entry. Fervently she hoped it would be the one she desired. She saw no sign of the man as she walked from the car park to the hotel entrance, and once inside she asked to use the house telephone as her excuse for being there. At the receptionist's friendly, 'Be our guest,' she closeted herself behind the glass door of the booth, and spent an interminable time riffling through the directory, pretending to make several calls. Her patience was rewarded when she finally emerged from the booth and peeped cautiously through a window facing the street, just in time to see the rear of the sports car speeding back along the way it had come.

'That's got rid of him for the moment, anyway,' she told herself with satisfaction. The Wheelback was too far away from Fullcote Hall for Gus Crawford to connect the two, but his mere presence in the district posed a threat that occupied her mind to the exclusion of everything else as she drove steadily back towards the Hall, keeping a wary eye on her driving mirror in case the sports car should reappear. It did not, and she rounded the shelter-belt of beeches at the front of the Hall with a distinct feeling of relief. It vanished abruptly when she pulled into her previous parking place beside the dovecote, and saw Zilla's car was still there.

'It's got a flat tyre.' Marion came out to greet her. 'Zilla didn't notice it until she got in to leave, and she doesn't carry a spare, so Greville invited her to stay.'

'Greville would!' Rane thought tartly, but she kept her feelings to herself, as cautiously she kept Gus Crawford's presence in the district to herself as well. If she mentioned that she had seen him, someone was bound to ask where, and she did not feel like explaining in front of Greville that she had stopped on 'their' pull-in. She found it difficult enough to explain the reason to herself, let alone to him.

'You're quiet, Rane?'

'I've got a bit of a headache.' The age-old excuse again, she thought wryly, but she smiled at Marion across the dinner table, grateful for the girl's concern. She would be even more concerned if she could know what occupied her thoughts. The image of Gus Crawford, and his reputation for leech-like persistence until he had worried every last detail out of a story, lay like a cloud between herself and the excellent dinner on her plate, until she scarcely noticed what it was she ate.

Her eyes noticed something else, which gave her even more food for thought. Idly they fixed on Zilla's hand across the table, attracted by the brilliants in her large and ostentatious ring. Abstractedly they followed the sparkle of light, then suddenly keened into alertness, riveted by the dark smudge that stained the gripping side of the mannequin's index finger.

So Zilla's 'puncture' wasn't an accident, after all! The mark, Rane felt certain, was a stain caused by a mixture of oil and road dirt pressed into the mannequin's beautifully kept hand when she unscrewed the wheel-cap and depressed the valve, releasing the air out of her tyre, and so securing for herself the coveted invitation from Greville to remain at the Hall. Against such ruthless determination, what chance had she? Rane's headache became a reality, and shadowed her eyes with an even deeper smudge that made valid her excuse to retire early.

'I'll go up as well, I'm still shivering from perching on that wretched wall this morning,' Marion complained.

'I want to do some work on the sketches for my Autumn Collection.' Leo joined the exodus, and sheer contrariness almost made Rane recant. She was playing right into Zilla's hands by leaving her alone with Greville. The smug smile on the other woman's face scored up her victory, and Rane hesitated, then shrugged.

'He's not worth fighting for,' she lied to herself robustly. The throbbing inside her head got worse by the minute, and the tears she would not allow to fall in the car threatened to spill over now, and if they did Zilla would gloat, Greville would sneer, and her pride as well as her heart would be in ribbons.

'Goodnight, everybody.'

Rane fled for her room. She passed the suit of armour in the hall without a second glance, and bundled herself into her nightdress with scant regard for its lacy delicacy, dropping into bed with a groan of relief that if she had allowed herself to think about it, would have become a sob.

She must have slept. The square of window in her room gave on to pitch darkness, and the illuminated hands of her travelling clock stood at something after one. She sat up in bed, uneasily aware that something had disturbed her. But what? She strained her ears and eyes in the darkness, but on the surface everything seemed to be perfectly normal. The wind still sang coldly round the corner of the old house. The doves still fluttered and fussed in the cote.

'Doves!' she exclaimed softly to herself. Doves shouldn't be making a fuss at this hour of the night. They ought to be asleep on their nest-boxes, or wherever. In a flash she was out of bed and hurrying to the window. Something—or someone—must have disturbed them.

Gus Crawford?

Even as the possibility flashed across her mind, her hand reached for her dressing gown. A cautious peep through the window showed nothing untoward on the ground below, but the attractive shrubbery flanking the dovecot was capable of hiding a dozen reporters with ease.

'If that newshound's followed me here, I'll give him a piece of my mind that'll penetrate even his thick skin!' she fumed. She slid her feet into mules and hurried to her bedroom door, noticing a light under Leo's door across the landing as she stepped outside. He must still be burning the gone-midnight oil, working on his new designs. For a moment Rane hesitated, then she crossed the landing and tapped softly on the wood.

'Leo?'

'Why, Rane, what's the matter? Are you ill?' The vivid pattern on Leo's dressing gown tempted her to answer in the affirmative, but she blinked and recovered and shook her head.

'Ill-tempered, more likely.' Keeping her voice low, she swiftly put Leo in the picture and the young designer frowned.

'You think this reporter fellow knows about my Summer Collection being photographed at Fullcote Hall?'

'Why else would he be in the district?' Rane demanded.

'I intend to find out,' Leo declared grimly.

'I'm coming with you.'

The stairs were a well of darkness, the hall a place of shadows, and the suit of armour gleamed ghostlike beside the door as Leo slid the bolts free.

'Be careful, we don't want to waken the whole household.' Rane tiptoed outside after the Frenchman, and gasped as the keen wind cut through her flimsy attire.

'Whoever it is must be close to the cote, to disturb the doves.'

'Somewhere in the shrubbery,' Rane hissed.

The shrubbery was productive of prickles, hidden roots that trapped her toes and tripped her up, and thin, whippy twigs that slapped painfully against her face in the darkness. And a cat.

'Oh, you gave me such a fright!' It curled round Rane's legs with an ingratiating purr, and she jumped violently at the unexpected contact.

'Steady!' Leo put his arm round her shoulders and pulled her upright as she stumbled over the small, furry body.

'I'll pick it up and take it back indoors with us. Puss! Puss! Where's it gone?'

A low, deep-throated growl told her *why* it had gone. A black shape, darker than the darkness, faced them with gleaming teeth and rumbling threats.

'Don't move, or the dog will attack. I intend to see who you are.'

A click, a brilliant swathe of light that dazzled her senses and blinded her eyes, and Greville's voice from the darkness immediately behind it, loaded with a menace far more terrifying than a dozen dogs.

'Greville,' she gasped. 'Thank goodness you've come!'

'From the look of things, it's a good job I came in time,' he retorted grimly. He stepped into the circle of his own torchlight, and his icy glance travelled significantly over Leo's gaudy dressing gown and her own flimsy wrap, and the Frenchman's arm still flung protectively across her shoulders.

'In time? In time for what?' For an electric second her stunned mind refused to credit his meaning. The second came to an end, as the meaning penetrated, and a scarlet tide of colour rushed from Rane's throat to her forehead. Words choked her. She opened her mouth and took in a lungful of wintry air.

'We came to find out what was disturbing the doves,' she spat back at him furiously. 'I tripped over a cat. If Leo hadn't caught me, I'd have fallen.'

'What cat?' Greville enquired flatly.

The dovecote had returned to its normal night-time peace, and she could not produce the cat. It had vanished, along with the credibility of her explanation.

'Are you suggesting . . .?' she began furiously, incensed by his manner.

'I'm suggesting we continue this conversation in my study,' Greville retorted coldly. 'In your state of dress,' his tone said, 'state of undress,' 'you'd be better indoors where it's warm.'

The last thing Rane felt she needed was warmth. Fury at his deliberate, insulting lack of understanding brought her temper to boiling point, and it spilled over when he reached out and grasped her by the arm.

'Take your hands off me!' she cried shrilly.

'Take your hands off her!' Greville took her own words and turned them on Leo, and his hand gripped her wrist with fingers of steel as the Frenchman's arm left her shoulders and dropped to his side.

'Come with me.'

She had no option. To try to break loose from

Greville's grip would be to invite an undignified struggle, which she was certain to lose. He did not speak again until they reached the house. The black retriever padded beside them, and Rane could hear Leo's footsteps bringing up the rear. They reached the hall, illuminated now, and Greville paused for a moment and rebolted the front door without loosing her arm. From somewhere on the landing above them Rane heard a door close softly, but she could not see which one, then Greville said, 'In here,' and propelled her ungently through a door on the opposite side of the hall from the dining room, and she forgot the closing door upstairs and tried unsuccessfully to calm the apprehension that rose in her as he thrust her into a chair and clicked on the large electric fire, then took up his stance beside it, looking accusingly down at her. With an effort she restrained an impulse to stretch her hands to the blessed warmth of the bright bars, and instead clasped them tightly together on her lap, trying to still their trembling, striving to retain some semblance of dignity—an impossibility, she discovered, when shivering in déshabille while confronting a hostile host who has the psychological advantage of still being fully clothed in immaculate evening dress.

Greville and Zilla must have sat up late together. The reason for Greville's attire added to her mental misery, and mounted further fuel to her rising anger as he waved Leo curtly to a chair beside her.

'Sit down.'

'I prefer to stand, thank you,' Leo returned stiffly, and irritably Rane wished the Frenchman would not try to sound quite so heroic. He was acting as if he was about to be blindfolded and stood against a wall and executed at dawn, an attitude that could hardly help their case with Greville now. To even appear to be on the defensive was tantamount to pleading guilty, she realised impatiently.

'*Sit down!*' This time Greville's tone brooked no refusal, and with a slightly surprised look on his face, Leo's knees buckled, and he sat.

'And now,' Greville straightened up from his leaning post against the mantel, and towered over them, and his voice cut with the icy edge of the east wind soughing round the house outside, 'and now, I want an explanation. From both of you.'

CHAPTER FIVE

'I'VE already given you one explanation.' Stubbornly, Rane refused to enlarge.

'So you admit there is another?'

'There *isn't* another explanation,' she denied furiously. 'If you're going to twist every word I say. . . .'

'Leo?'

Greville cut across her tirade, questioning her explanation, demanding one from Leo to see if the two matched.

'Rane came to my room,' the Frenchman began.

'*Did* she?' Greville interposed grimly. 'Go on.'

'It wasn't like that at all,' Rane butted in forcefully. His tone tried, condemned, and sentenced her in one short breath, and she would endure it in silence no longer. She found her feet and her voice in a dual flash of fury, and justified herself in ringing tones.

'It wasn't like that at all!'

'Like what?'

'Like your nasty, suspicious mind thinks it was,' she flashed back, beside herself with anger at the inference of his attitude. 'Even a criminal isn't convicted without a hearing,' she declared hotly.

'I'm listening.'

Doubtless he expected her to be grateful for that. She had to exert all her willpower to check the flow of angry words that tumbled to the edge of her tongue, but somehow she curbed them and gritted out through tight lips,

'The doves disturbed me. They were fluttering

about in their cote, so something, or someone, must have disturbed them, and after bumping into Gus Crawford of the *Echo* on my way back from the camera shop this evening. . . .'

'Did you hear the doves?' Greville enquired of Leo. 'No, I. . . .'

'Did you know about this reporter fellow from the *Echo*?'

'No, I. . . .'

'Will you be quiet, and listen to me?' Rane shouted in exasperation. 'Leo didn't know about either of them until I told him. I heard the doves. I told you, their fluttering about in the cote woke me up, and I was going out by myself to investigate, to see what was wrong, when I saw a light under Leo's bedroom door and realised he must still be awake, so I decided it would be more sensible if the two of us went together, in case it was Crawford, and he gave trouble.'

'It seems to me you were inviting trouble, going out dressed as you are now.'

Rane's face flamed. In the heat of her anger against Greville she had, for the moment, forgotten the flimsy nature of her negligee. With an outraged tug she pulled her wrap more tightly round her, unthinkingly emphasising the slender curves of her dainty figure, and the grey eyes kindled, but Rane was too furious to give them heed.

'There was only one place where anyone could hide by the dovecote, and that was in the shrubbery.' With her chin held high she swept aside his comment, and ignored the sense behind it. In her haste to discover the cause of the disturbance, she had not paused to consider the possible consequences of her impulsive action, if indeed she had come across an intruder. 'All we discovered was a cat,' she ended tautly, 'and that tripped me up. Leo's arm saved me from falling.'

'There *was* a cat,' Leo confirmed lamely.

Rane silenced him with a withering look. His support had come too late. The gauntlet was down between herself and Greville, and she would wield her own bludgeon.

'We hadn't been outside for more than five minutes before you came along with your torch and the dog,' she declared roundly, 'so what brought you out there?' She turned the tables on her questioner and hurled one back at him.

'You'd been out there for exactly eight and a half minutes when I caught up with you,' Greville informed her, and Rane stared at him.

'You must have followed us,' she realised. 'Spied on us!' she hissed furiously.

'On the contrary...'

'How else do you know so precisely the amount of time we spent outside?'

'Quite simply,' Greville retorted. 'After a certain hour each evening the house doors are locked, and after that, if anyone leaves the house, an alarm bell rings in my room.'

After eleven o'clock.... So that was the reason for Greville's curfew, why he had asked her if she intended to go out again after she retired on the night of her arrival. Rane's opinion of the security system at Fullcote Hall did a rapid about-turn. It appeared to be comparable with Fort Knox.

'If I'd known you were so well guarded I wouldn't have put myself out to investigate,' she said coldly. 'And now,' she drew herself up, briefly envying Zilla the height that allowed her to be haughty, 'and now, since you've had the explanation you asked for....' He did not ask, he demanded, and he patently did not believe the explanation when it was given. 'I'll return to my room and sleep safe in the knowledge that you'll be here on guard,' she declared sarcastically, relegating her host to the same level as the retriever that lay across the rug at his feet. With an independent toss of her head she turned to sweep past him towards the door. Nothing could make her flimsy negligee swish with the dignity of a satin gown, nothing could give her the coveted extra inches that would turn her exit into a triumph, but she made the most of what she had. Her proudly uptilted chin gave her the illusion of extra height, and successfully prevented her from seeing the dog's tail jutting out across her path from beside Greville's feet.

'Don't step on Chip.'

She stepped, and the retriever got up and moved hurriedly out of range, and her mules slipped on the polished parquet floor.

'I warned you to be careful.'

For the second time in an hour, male arms reached out and grasped her, and prevented her from falling ignominiously flat on her face, only this time the arms were older, more mature. More experienced? Arms that had, perhaps, recently held Zilla in their clasp? Rane flinched away from their hard, remembered strength, the steel muscles disturbingly close through her flimsy gown, close enough to feel the wild, erratic beating of her heart that seemed to stop at his first touch, then raced ahead so fast that it became an unendurable pain. Rane closed her eyes against the agony, and swayed against him, hearing his voice cut sharply through a darkening mist.

'Did you hurt your ankle when you slipped?'

Her heart felt as if it was breaking in two, and Greville was concerned in case she had sprained her ankle! The bitter irony of it caught her by the throat, and she wanted to laugh hyserically at the sick humour of it, then just as suddenly she wanted to weep.

'No. No, not much. I think I can walk on it.' The words came out in a strangled gasp, and she put up her hands to push his arms away, and only she knew what it cost her to try. She raised her eyes, dark with mute appeal, to his, and straightaway became lost in their grey, fathomless depths. She forgot Leo. She forgot the dog. She felt her anger begin to slip away, and with it her only defence against Greville, leaving her rawly exposed to his compelling magnetism that drew her unresisting into the encircling band of his arms.

'Don't walk on it again tonight.'

The words were a warning, they were not spoken out of consideration for her ankle. Instantly Rane stiffened away from him, an angry flush staining her cheeks and giving her hands the courage this time to push his arms away. Her heart wept that his arms were willing to be pushed away, otherwise her strength alone would not suffice. They dropped to his sides, and she stood bereft, and lest her lack of courage should shame her she spun away from him while she could still summon the willpower, and retorted,

'The only place it'll need to carry me tonight is back to bed!'

It carried her to the study door at a run. She felt Greville's eyes like twin daggers boring into her retreating back, and all plans for a dignified exit fled as she wrenched panting at the heavy knob, using both hands because one of her own was too small to twist it unaided. They slipped on the smooth surface, and she felt her palms wet with perspiration, but to wipe them dry would be to betray the depths of her agitation to Greville, and with gritted teeth she tightened her grip and wrenched again, and this time the knob turned, and she flung the door ajar and dived through the opening like a hunted creature dives into the safety of its burrow. With a sob of relief she gained the hall and pulled the door to behind her with a jerk that nearly dislocated her shoulder. With scant regard for her ankle she lifted her negligee clear of her feet and took the stairs two at a time, not risking a backwards glance until she gained the landing outside her own room door.

Greville's bedroom door was open, she saw, and so was Leo's, and a widening crack of light from the hall below showed the study door was about to follow suit. An accented French voice bade Greville a curt goodnight, and Rane did not wait to hear any more. Heedless of the risk she took of banging her toes against unseen furniture, she stumbled across her darkened room and into bed, where she pulled the clothes high over her shoulders and listened with straining ears as steps sounded on the stairs. Leo's. She heard his bedroom door close, then Greville's voice spoke from the hall below, saying something to his dog. More footsteps on the stairs. She tensed. They paused outside her door, and time stood still, while she held her breath until it felt as if her lungs must burst for want of air, then the steps continued on along the landing, and a second later Greville's room door closed, and only the pale starlight was left to witness the heaving blankets that covered Rane's violently trembling form.

'Rane! Rane, are you awake?'

'I'm half dressed. What is it?'

Leo's voice sounded violently agitated, even for the excitable Frenchman, and Rane hastily tugged a slip over her pants and bra and reached for her wrap with a feeling that this had all happened before. She hurried across the room and pulled open the door, remembering that it had all happened, in reverse, only a few hours ago.

'What on earth's the matter?'

'My sketches. They're gone!' Leo's face was chalk-white, and his hair stood up in spiky disarray from where his frantic fingers raked through its blond length.

'Your Autumn Collection? They can't be missing! You were working on them in your room last night, when I knocked on your door,' Rane expostulated. 'You must have put down your portfolio somewhere and forgotten where you left it.'

'They've gone, I tell you!'

'Let me come in and have a look.' Rane thrust down a pang of foreboding, and tried to make her voice sound brisk and practical. Leo was forgetful, but he had never to her knowledge been this careless before, and her eyes skimmed across his disordered room with anxious speed.

'Here's your portfolio.' A wave of relief passed over her at another crisis averted. 'You must have left it here when you came downstairs with me last night.' She reached out her hand and withdrew the familiar cover from underneath a pile of miscellaneous socks, ties and underwear of the same lurid colouring as his dressing gown.

'I know where the portfolio is.' Leo waxed impatient at her obtuseness. 'I told you, the *sketches* are missing.'

With a sinking heart, Rane remembered. She should have taken more heed of his exact words, knowing that his careful English would not use one word when he meant another.

'Some of your sketches are here,' her riffling fingers still clung on to one last faint hope.

'The Harvest Designs are gone!'

Rane's fingers ceased their riffling, and she stared at the Frenchman, apalled. The Harvest Designs! A collection within a collection, and the cream of his new work.

'I was working on them when you knocked on my door last night,' Leo confirmed. 'I had them on the table here,' he indicated a small occasional table beside an easy chair, opposite to the bedroom door. A scatter of sketching materials still lay across its polished top. 'After I came back upstairs I didn't return to the table. The papers still lay across it as they are now, and there was nothing to indicate that they'd been disturbed. I switched off the light and went to bed.'

'So you didn't notice some of the sketches were missing until . . .?'

'Until a few minutes ago, just before I knocked on your door,' Leo finished for her distractedly. 'I went to put them into the portfolio with the others, before I got dressed.'

'Have you searched . . .?'

'Everywhere. But everywhere,' Leo groaned, and Rane believed him. The bedroom looked as if a hurricane had hit it, with drawers pulled out and cushions scattered on the carpet.

'This can only be Gus Crawford,' Rane said quietly.

'But how . . .?'

'Last night, when we went outside together, did you shut the front door behind us?' she asked him urgently.

'No, why? I left it open, ready for when we returned.'

'It would be easy enough for Crawford to recognise you by your accent,' Rane warmed to her theory. 'And it would need only seconds for him to slip inside the door and upstairs, the moment we were out of sight. He couldn't miss seeing which was your room, and the rest would be easy. He'd tuck the sketches in his pocket and be away before we even got to the shrubbery.'

'We must find him—pursue him!'

'Before we do anything, I'm going to wake Greville and let him know what's going on.'

'I'm already awake, and I *insist* upon knowing what's going on.'

Greville blocked the doorway, formidable in hacking jacket and breeches, his face wind whipped to freshness from his early morning ride, and his eyes were as glacial as that same wind. He spoke, and his voice made the wind seem warm by comparison.

'Last night I was tempted to check and make certain you'd both adjourned to separate rooms after you left my study,' he told Rane icily, 'but I gave you the benefit of the doubt.'

'How dare you!' So that was why his footsteps had paused outside her bedroom door. 'It's absolutely monstrous of you to suggest. . . .' Her eyes blazed green fire, from a face from which all vestige of colour had fled, and she turned on him like a tiny tigress, quivering from head to toe with outrage. 'Leo came to tell me that some of his sketches are missing,' she hissed upwards into Greville's face. 'I was already nearly dressed when he knocked on my door.' Too angry for false modesty, Rane opened her wrap briefly to prove how nearly she had been dressed, then pulled it back round her with a furious tug. 'If you still don't believe me, go and put your hand in my bed, you'll find the bedclothes are still warm,' she challenged him fiercely.

'That won't be necessary,' Greville said stiffly. 'I'm prepared to accept. . . .'

'I'm not prepared to accept your unpleasant insinuations,' Rane flared. 'The least you can do is to apologise!'

'Apologies? Insinuations? What do these things matter?' Leo's arm's waved in a windmill of desperation. 'I tell you, my sketches are missing— gone!' he cried dramatically.

'Sketches can't walk away on their own,' Greville cut short his histrionics with an impatient gesture.

'They've probably walked as far as the *Echo* by now, in Gus Crawford's pocket,' lamented their distracted owner.

'How would this reporter fellow know where you kept them?' Greville demanded. 'There's no reason to suppose he's even aware that you're staying at Fullcote Hall. Unless——' he paused and his eyes narrowed, and a shiver started up Rane's spine as they came to rest upon her, transfixing her with a look of blistering contempt, 'unless he gained the knowledge from one of your own number here.'

There was no doubt of his meaning, nor of his opinion of such treachery. Rane went cold, then hot— blazing hot with anger at such an unjust assumption.

'That's an infamous thing to say!' she cried. 'Why should I, of all people, do such a thing?'

'By your own admission you met Crawford on your way back to Fullcote yesterday afternoon.' He made the meeting sound like an assignation, and Rane's sorely tried temper gave way.

'I didn't know I should bump into Gus Crawford. How could I?' she cried shrilly. 'I didn't know myself that I should have to go into town to get my camera mended.'

'You damaged your camera with your own hand. Very conveniently,' Greville reminded her significantly, and Rane felt sick. The flash of temper that had caused the damage was costing her dear, not only in having to pay for her camera. Her own injured image could not be repaired so easily, and was

probably damaged for ever in Greville's eyes. All of a
sudden, a great weariness descended upon her, and
her shoulders drooped, while the anger that sustained
her against him vanished, to leave her feeling empty
and drained.

'You must think of me whatever you choose.' Her
voice was flat, but it held a quiet dignity that was more
impressive than any show of anger. She was too far
gone to either know or care what impression she might
create, and went on with determined steadiness, 'Gus
Crawford's presence in the area is no doing of mine.
I didn't meet him by previous arrangement, in fact I
did all I could to throw him off my trail.' Briefly she
detailed the steps she had taken, and which she
thought at the time were successful, and finished
emphatically, 'and I did *not* tell Crawford, either
directly or indirectly, of Leo's presence at Fullcote
Hall, nor of what he was doing here. Secrecy in that
respect is as important to *Dress* as it is to the designers
themselves.'

'In that case, in view of what's happened I assume
you'll suspend operations here now?' There was
undisguised satisfaction in Greville's voice, and both
Leo and Rane stared at him in stunned surprise.

'Suspend operations? *Non! Non!* To stop now, it is
impossible!'

'Quite impossible,' Rane backed up Leo's statement
emphatically. 'Leo needs the publicity, and I've got a
printing deadline to meet.' It helped, she discovered,
to think about printing deadlines. Mundane, everyday
urgencies that, no matter what the state of her own
personal feelings, must be met and dealt with. It also
helped, she discovered with a sense of malicious
satisfaction, to defy Greville on his own ground, this
time ably supported by Leo.

'Please yourself.' Their host shrugged off the matter

as of supreme unimportance to him, and Rane's lips tightened. 'I don't see how you can possibly go hunting this Crawford fellow, and keep to your modelling schedule at the same time.'

'Somehow, it shall be done.'

'We shan't need to go hunting anybody,' Rane said definitely, and answered Leo's immediate protest with, 'If Gus Crawford's got your sketches, they're as good as lost already. They'll be splashed across the fashion page of tomorrow's *Echo* for the whole world to see,' she pointed out with cruel truth.

'But my Harvest Collection. . . .'

'Has already been gathered,' Rane retorted bluntly. 'Count it as lost, Leo, and design some more clothes. Even better ones. It's the only way to beat Crawford at his own game.' The light of battle was back in her eyes. Fighting Gus Crawford was infinitely easier than fighting Greville, because she did not also have to fight herself.

'If it *is* Crawford who's got them,' Greville interjected.

His comment rasped like sandpaper on Rane's raw nerves as she wriggled into her working gear of slacks, sweater and duffle coat, and prepared to do battle with the long day ahead. That it would be a battle she was soon left in no doubt.

'We'll do the yellow broderie anglaise sundress first, with Marion,' Leo announced. 'The picnic scene under the beech trees, with the lake and the punt in the background,' he enlarged, regaining his enthusiasm.

'I shan't have to raise my camera too high,' Rane warned him. 'The scene's supposed to be shot in high summer, and there aren't any leaves on the beech trees yet.'

'Marion will be missing, as well as the leaves,'

Greville stated calmly, and added in the speaking silence that followed his bombshell, 'She woke this morning with a heavy cold.' His tone said, 'What can you expect after making her sit on a garden wall in the teeth of an east wind yesterday?'

'I've told her she must remain in bed for at least a couple of days,' he added casually. 'She's nineteen in a few days' time, and I don't want her to spoil her birthday by feeling ill.' His whole attitude emphasised his authority over his ward, and his ascendancy over Leo, resurrecting the bone of contention between them, and Rane groaned inwardly. The day looked like becoming even more nerve-racking than the previous one. And with Marion ill, that left only Zilla, who patently was not the sundress-and-picnic-under-the-trees type. Leo obviously thought so, too, and about-faced with an adroitness that roused Rane's admiration.

'In that case, we'll use Zilla, and the carriage you promised to lend us.'

'Touché!' Rane murmured under her breath, and slanted a quick glance at Greville, but his face remained sphinxlike, registering no emotion. 'He'd make an excellent poker player,' she decided crossly, piqued that the combined forces of herself and Leo had so signally failed to put him out of countenance.

'The carriage is ready, Mr York.'

'Thank you, Jack.' Whatever his attitude to his guests, Greville was always scrupulously polite to his staff. Rane scored a reluctant point in his favour, and gathered her equipment together with a feeling of relief that the action of the day was about to begin.

'Where's Zilla?' She, too, was missing, and Rane frowned impatiently.

'Gone upstairs to change,' Leo answered. 'Ah, here she is.' A door shut overhead. The sound teased a chord in Rane's memory, and she saw Greville's head raise, then she forgot everything as Zilla appeared at the head of the wide, curved staircase, and started to descend. No prima donna could have made a more impressive entrance. Rane wondered, cynically, if the mannequin had peeped out of her room first to make sure they were all, including Greville, gathered together in the hall to witness her performance, then professionalism thrust every other consideration aside, and she dropped to one knee on the polished floor and raised her camera.

'Hold it!'

It was a picture she could not miss. It was a picture which, from her deliberate pose, Zilla was determined she should not miss. The low-cut strapless evening gown in wine-dark velvet, with a floating panel lined with self-coloured moiré silk like a miniature train dropping to the stair at her back; her pale arms, pearl-like against the dark material, her one hand resting languidly on the polished hand rail; her hair piled into a chignon on top of her head, emphasising the high cheekbones and the lustrous black eyes, relieved only by a choker of brilliants at her throat—Zilla was regal in her elegance. With a thumb and forefinger of her other hand, she held delicately to the mandarin collar of a duster coat of the same moiré silk as the lining of her dress panel, allowing its shining folds to spread softly across the stair at her feet.

'*Magnifique!*'

Leo meant the dress, and not the mannequin, and Rane stifled a gurgle of amusement as a scowl of temper momentarily distorted the perfect features, and Zilla broke her pose and recommenced her gliding walk to the hall. Rane transferred her attention from her camera to Greville, and a pang shot through her at the rapt expression on his face. His eyes were narrowed in the way Rane remembered so well, as he watched the mannequin descend to the hall and glide to his side, complacently aware that she was receiving his sole attention.

'Magnificent, indeed,' he echoed Leo, and his praise, Rane had no doubt, was for the wearer and not for the dress. She turned away with suddenly blurred vision.

'This ensemble was to be photographed with the carriage as a background, not the staircase.' From behind her, Rane heard Zilla's sharp voice criticising her for wasting time and film on a useless shot that she herself had deliberately provoked, and with difficulty Rane curbed an angry retort. Zilla was quite correct, Leo *had* planned to use the carriage, but it was a wrong decision, terribly wrong. Rane knew it the moment she walked outside and stood on top of the stone entrance steps, and saw the sleek coach-built landau drawn up on the gravel below. Its black paintwork glowed with Jack's promised polish, the brass side lanterns sparkled in the March sunshine, and a pair of perfectly matched greys stood quietly in the shafts, with Jack at their heads.

'It should be a bride stepping out of a carriage like that, not someone in ordinary evening dress,' Rane exclaimed impulsively, slandering the lovely wine velvet. 'Imagine, white lace, reflected in the polished black paintwork.' She turned to the designer eagerly. 'This is your chance, Leo. Don't you see? Design a bridal gown, and forget your Harvest Collection.'

'But it was my best work yet.'

'This will be your best work *ever*,' Rane retorted excitedly. 'Think of a bride,' she urged, and knew he would instantly think of Marion. From the way his face lit up, she knew he *was* thinking of Marion, that he had tuned in to her own inspired wavelength, and was bewitched by the music he heard there.

'Gus Crawford did you a good turn by removing your Harvest Collection designs last night,' she went on enthusiastically.

'They were an inspiration,' their hapless owner groaned.

A wedding gown would be inspired by love. Rane swam against a wave of desolation, and broke surface to hear Zilla ask sharply,

'What's this about Gus Crawford?'

'We think he was prowling about outside, after dark last night,' Rane answered her shortly. At the time, Zilla could only just have parted company from Greville, so she could not possibly have been asleep, and consequently must have heard the commotion when they all came back indoors, and it would be uncharacteristic of her, to say the least, if she had not made it her business to discover the reason for the disturbance. 'This morning, the Harvest Collection sketches were missing.' Curtly, Rane relayed information which she was convinced was not news to Zilla.

'Leo won't have time to design an entire new range,' the mannequin objected forcefully.

'He will. He must!' Rane turned to the Frenchman, and elation seized her as she saw the glow of enthusiasm that transfigured the thin, nervous features. 'You've got nearly a month to the actual showing,' she persisted eagerly. 'Pull out all the stops, Leo, and design a new collection. I'll attend to the photographic sessions here for you.'

'I won't model clothes unless Leo's present to make sure everything's perfect. I insist on you keeping to the schedule!' Zilla stormed, her eyes snapping with temper as she saw the star attraction of Leo's Autumn Collection slipping out of her grasp. She was to have modelled the Harvest Collection. It was obvious, even to the uninitiated, that Zilla's sultry sophistication was unsuitable to model a bridal dress designed for and inspired by a nineteen-year-old.

'I demand that the carriage be used as a background for this evening dress, as we originally planned,' Zilla cried angrily. 'It's the perfect foil for the wine velvet.'

'You're in no position to demand anything of the kind.' Rane lost her patience. 'I decide what photographs are to be published in *Dress*, and if you won't co-operate, I'll take the shots I need without you.' Aggressively she asserted her right to decide on the contents of the publication she represented. 'Anyone with the slightest imagination would see that the carriage is crying out to hold a bride in white,' she finished positively. Her own imagination was a torment that made the world suddenly swim in front of her eyes. Her breath became a pain, and her knees a weakness that demanded somewhere to sit before her legs folded under her. The nearest seat was the hide upholstery of the landau, and she stumbled towards it, groping her way through the opened door, and pulling herself up into the carriage with a heartfelt wish that Jack had left the hood up instead of down, so exposing her to Zilla's spiteful glare and the keen, probing look of Greville's narrowed eyes. She discounted Leo. His face held a faraway expression, and he burst out suddenly,

'Tiered lace! That's it—tiered lace! I go to start on it now. This instant!'

'And I'm going to change back into my own clothes until the rest of you come to your senses!' With a flounce that held none of the dignity of her entrance, Zilla vanished through the door after the designer. It closed with a resounding slam, and Rane leaned back limply against the buttoned hide upholstery and closed her eyes. This was where the bride would sit. But not how the bride would feel. Tears pricked behind her closed lids as gravel crunched beside the landau, the carriage rocked, and her eyes flew open, over-bright, and fixed themselves on Greville as he leaned back comfortably in the seat beside her.

'Let them go, Jack.' He signalled to the groom, who promptly mounted the box, the reins held lightly in his capable hands, and clicked his tongue to the horses once, twice, and as if in a dream Rane felt the carriage begin to move.

'What . . .?' She sat bolt upright in the seat, and turned towards the now closed door, and instantly Greville's hands reached out and grasped her round the waist, pulling her back and holding her easily against him.

'If the landau's to be used for so important a person as a bride, we must at least give it a trial run,' he remarked wickedly.

Nothing could be further from bridal finery than her own workaday clothes, Rane thought shakily. She was in much-used slacks and sweater; she was in a duffle coat and flat-heeled shoes. And, inescapably, she was in Greville's arms. For a moment of stunned shock she remained still, then the moment and the shock passed, and realisation returned, and with it a frantic need to escape, and she began to struggle ineffectually to free herself.

'Loose me,' she begged him desperately. 'Let me go. What on earth will Jack think, if he sees . . .?'

'Jack's eyes are on the greys, and a landau doesn't boast a driving mirror.' There was laughter in Greville's voice, laughter in his grey eyes, and an infectious gaiety in the humming wheels as they turned off the gravel and spun at a spanking pace along the smooth tarmac road that circled the estate.

'Where are we going?' Rane discovered she did not care. The turbulent emotions of the last twenty-four hours had left her weak and vulnerable, her defences in disarray, and totally unprepared for Greville's unexpected action. Hooves clip-clopped in mesmeric rhythm in front of her, the wind sang a siren song of enchantment in her ears, and Greville's hand reached up and drew back the hood of her duffle coat away from her flushed face, and allowed his seeking lips to find, and capture, her own.

CHAPTER SIX

THE bridal finery was missing, but all the emotions were there. The touch of Greville's lips upon her mouth transported Rane into realms of ecstasy, his fingers teasing her curls sent a thrill of rapture coursing through her veins that set her pulses leaping like the lambs in the parkland on either side of the carriage. From somewhere overhead a lark trilled, invisible in the sunlit blue, the high sweet notes dropping through the clear air like golden rain, to find an echo in her singing heart.

It was a dream, a delirium, and somewhere deep inside her a voice of caution warned her that the dream would fade, and the fever subside, and the awakening would bring bitter regret, and pain. But the wild siren singing enslaved her, Greville's arms enchained her, and Rane threw caution to the winds and gave herself up to the sweet folly of the moment, helpless to resist as eagerly she returned kiss for kiss with an ardour to match his own.

'Shall I take them through the gates, Mr York, or stay on the park road?'

A voice spoke from another world, invading the bright, shimmering bubble of her own. Bitterly Rane resented the voice, wished it would go away, but it insisted, demanding to be answered.

'Mr York?'

The carriage slowed as the stone pillars of the entrance gates loomed closer, and Greville spoke, his voice uttering prosaic instructions.

'Keep to the park road.'

The bubble burst, scattering the bright shining colours into grey nothingness. The lark stopped singing with characteristic suddenness, as if somebody had turned off a switch, and Greville unlinked his arms from about her, releasing her, while Rane slumped back, free in the seat, and stared with unseeing eyes at the passing green as Jack obediently turned the greys and pointed them back towards the Hall, and a cold numbness settled on her heart that had nothing to do with the March wind and everything to do with the pain that was yet to come.

'Will the carriage serve your purpose as a background to Leo's bridal design?'

If only the circumstances were different, it would more than serve her own purpose. The pain arrived, piercing knifelike through the numbness. Through stiff lips she managed to answer,

'It'll serve beautifully.'

It would serve another bride's dress, another bride. With all her heart Rane longed to be that bride, to wear that dress, and knew that it would never be. How could she bear to photograph another bride, in the place she would give her own life to occupy?

'Allow me.'

Jack drew the greys to a halt in front of the Hall entrance, and Greville sprang down from the carriage and with a mocking bow offered Rane his arm, parodying the action of a gallant bridegroom. The knife twisted in her heart, and she caught her breath at the sharp agony of it. With stony eyes she stared at his hand, held up to assist her from the carriage. The hurt of it went too deep for tears, and dumbly she supposed she ought to be thankful for that; at least dry eyes prevented her from betraying her weakness to Greville. Let him think her eager response to his lovemaking was a passing whim, and nothing more, just as it was to him. With slow deliberation she gathered her camera from where it had fallen unheeded to the back of the seat, and gathered together her courage to enable her to rest her fingers lightly upon Greville's sleeve. Oh, the exquisite agony of it, to set aside his mockery and join in his play-acting, to step down to the gravel beside him, commenting lightly in what she hoped would pass muster as a professional sounding voice,

'It should photograph well. The polish Jack's put on the paintwork will act like a mirror to a white dress.' From some untapped source of willpower she dredged up a smile in praise of the groom's efforts.

'Talking of photographs, Miss Strickland,' a flattered Jack turned to look down at her from his high seat on the box, 'if you need to take any more pictures of the dovecote with that branch of almond blossom resting across the front of the nest-box holes, will you take it today, otherwise the branch won't be there.'

'Oh, what a shame!' Rane exclaimed. 'It looks so pretty with the white doves perched among the blossom.'

'The ginger tomcat from the stable yard uses the branch to perch on, too,' Jack replied without humour. 'With your permission, Mr York, I intend to saw off the branch as soon as I've brushed down the greys and put the carriage away. The cat's using it to gain entrance to the cote. It must have been there again last night, I found another dove badly clawed this morning. It was a sitting hen, too. That's the second in a week,' the groom counted savagely.

'So there *was* a cat!' Rane burst out. Jack's innocent remarks brought back all the suspicion, all the disbelief and tension of last night, and all the anger too, and dispelled any euphoria lingering from their carriage drive. 'I told you there was a cat!' She turned hard eyes on Greville. 'I said I heard a commotion in the dovecote!' He had not believed that, either, and unmercifully she turned the tables on his disbelief, vindicated by the lips of his own groom.

'Saw off the branch by all means. Do whatever you think's necessary.' Calmly Greville ignored her fierce justification, refusing to commit himself even in the face of irrefutable evidence. Giving the groom permission to destroy the picturesque pink froth of blossom without first asking if she might need it for any more background shots.

'You might at least have asked me if I wanted to take any more shots first, before Jack gets to work with his saw.' She forced her much shorter legs to unnatural activity to keep up with Greville's easy stride up the entrance steps. Breathlessly she trotted after him, her wrath rising with each hurrying step. 'You might have asked,' she panted.

'The doves need peace while they're nesting. It's important that they're not disturbed.'

The doves were important, and she was not. Wearily Rane felt she needed peace as well as the doves. She needed Greville even more, and was denied either.

'I was right about the cat.' Stubbornly she determined that Greville should admit her rightness.

'I believe you—about the cat.' An almost imperceptible pause in the middle of the sentence, that far from being the admission Rane sought, gave his words an insulting implication, and her eyes sparked angrily.

Greville believed her about the cat, but not about Gus Crawford. He still suspected that she and Leo. . . . With an effort she curbed an angry retort as a trim housemaid came towards them as they crossed the hall.

'I've put a copy of this morning's *Echo* on the desk in your study, Mr York.'

'The *Echo*, of course, Leo's designs will be front page news this morning,' Rane remembered bitterly. Now Greville would have to believe her. She followed him as he turned towards his study door, and was hard on his heels as he entered, determined to be with him when he opened the newspaper, and see for herself what Crawford had made of the stolen sketches. Determined to make Greville admit. . . .

'It's not on the front page,' he remarked.

'Try the fashion articles on the women's page inside.' Rane squirmed with impatience as he leafed through the newspaper, pausing to glance at a picture here, a headline there, until she could have screamed with frustration at his slowness. 'It's bound to be the main theme in the dress section.'

It was not. Far from being the main theme, Leo's designs were not even given a mention.

'Let me see.' Rane stood on tiptoe and craned her head disbelievingly over his forearm, the better to scan the page to make absolutely sure, uneasily remembering Greville's parting shot in Leo's bedroom, 'If it *is* Crawford who's got them. . . .'

But if it was not Gus Crawford who stole the designs, then—who? The disturbance in the dovecote had been accounted for by the presence of the cat, and she was willing to admit her excursion last night had been a wild goose chase. Nevertheless it did not alter the fact that the designs were missing, and Crawford was in the district, and he would not have left London unless he had some specific purpose in mind.

'Gus Crawford *is* in the locality,' she insisted, 'and it can only be Leo's Summer Collection that's drawn him here. Why else would he, of all people, come to a—a——' she stopped.

'A dead-and-alive place like this?'

'From Crawford's point of view, yes,' Rane retorted defensively. From her own, she would be content to spend the rest of her days in the loveliness of the Chiltern Hills, but, 'It's a far cry from Crawford's usual haunts,' she said briefly.

'I can imagine.' Greville's tone was dry. 'But given that it wasn't d'Arvel's world-shattering brilliance that brought him here. . . .'

'There's no need to be sarcastic about Leo's work,' Rane snapped. 'His sketches are still missing, so someone must have thought they were worth stealing.'

'Leaving that aside for the moment. . . .'

'*Only* for the moment,' Rane countered straightly.

'There's a much larger carrot at Fullcote Hall that might tempt an *Echo* reporter to venture into the wilds, if he got wind of it,' Greville spoke thoughtfully, ignoring her riposte. 'Or, to be more exact, carat,' he finished meaningly.

'Carat? I don't understand.' Rane looked up at him perplexedly. Greville was talking in riddles, when he should be raising the household to search for Leo's sketches if he was so sure the *Echo* reporter had not stolen them.

'Diamonds,' her host replied succinctly. 'To be precise, one particular diamond.' With swift steps he strode to the door, looked briefly outside, then shut it again and turned the key in the lock before returning to her side. 'Have you still got your camera with you?' he asked her à propos nothing.

'Yes, why?' he was still talking in riddles, and irritation rode Rane at her inability to solve them.

'I'd like you to do something for me. Take a photograph.'

She had already taken one photograph, but it was of him, not for him, and the memory of the circumstances in which it was taken made her voice sharp as she answered him noncommittally.

'A photograph of what?'

'A diamond,' he answered her casually, and Rane's eyes widened as he turned towards a high rolltop desk placed against the far wall of the room, and slid his fingers along the carved side of it, and immediately a large watercolour on the wall above it slid smoothly away to reveal a businesslike-looking safe door underneath. Greville reached up and twiddled for a moment with deft fingers until there was a faint click, and the safe door swung open to allow access to his hand.

'Is *that* a diamond?' Childish disappointment rode Rane's voice as she regarded the dull object which Greville held out towards her on a black velvet tray, and momentarily a smile flickered across his well cut lips.

'That's a diamond,' he confirmed gravely, and added, 'in the raw, of course, the crystal's still embedded in its host rock.'

'May I see?' Curiosity overcame Rane's antagonism and she held out her hand, and without hesitation Greville placed the tray and its precious contents in her palm.

'It's heavy. That's the rock it's encased in, I suppose.'

'The rock's kimberlite.'

'Where does it come from?'

'This particular crystal was found in one of the South African diamond fields.' Greville lowered himself on to the edge of a nearby table, which brought him satisfactorily closer to Rane's own height, and he answered her question readily enough, and a small ray of warmth stole into the cold numbness around her heart, that encased it like the kimberlite around the diamond and made it feel as cold, and as heavy. The diamond crystal, for all its disappointing dullness, was the most precious thing in the world, she decided, not for the market value that the world might place upon it, but because it gave herself and Greville common ground on which they could talk, freely and uninhibited by the tensions and strains with which their normal conversations were fraught. By handing over the diamond for her to look at, Greville had tacitly invited her to step with him on to the common ground, and eagerly Rane stepped, wishing the diamond were a crystal ball that she could gaze into, and then felt glad it was not, for fear that what it might show of her future would spoil the joy of the present moments, more wonderful by far to her than the nature's wonder which she balanced in her palm.

'It's large.' Rane inspected the crystal curiously.

'It's the largest flawless crystal to come out of its particular field this century,' Greville answered with immense satisfaction. 'Our agent was lucky to be on hand at the time, otherwise it might have been lost to us. There's fierce competition for a stone of this calibre, and the size and perfection of this one makes it extremely rare. A find like this makes news headlines once it becomes known.'

'Is that why you think Gus Crawford . . .?'

'Might have heard a whisper on the grapevine, and come in search of a story,' Greville finished for her. 'I brought the crystal to Fullcote Hall rather than leave it in our business premises in the city, in order to preserve secrecy as to its whereabouts in this country until we've had it cut and set. If the press here gets wind of its whereabouts, their headlines might attract even more unwelcome attention from elsewhere,' he predicted significantly. 'The security system at Fullcote is the best available, but I prefer not to have it put to the test by an expert safe breaker, if I can possibly help it,' he added drily.

'And you want me to photograph it for identification purposes, just in case?' Rane realised aloud.

'That's it,' Greville agreed. 'It's our usual practice to have every gem photographed before and after it's cut, and when it's finally set, but if I send for my man to do it here, his presence out of London might cause unwelcome conjecture which I'd prefer to avoid if possible. The Gus Crawfords of this world have ears as sharp as their eyes,' he concluded wryly. 'And since you're in situ. . . .' He paused, and waited.

'I'll make a bargain with you.' This was her opportunity, and Rane seized it unrepentantly. 'You help Leo to look for his design sketches, and I'll photograph your gemstone. Not otherwise,' she stated categorically, and stared Greville straight in the eye with a steely determination equal to his own. It was an advantage, she discovered gleefully, to be able to stare him straight in the eye. Usually she had to tilt her head right back to look up into his face, and she took instant advantage of the unexpected opportunity while he was sitting down, and his eyes were on a level with her own.

They regarded her steadily, with an unwavering grey stare, measuring her determination, weighing her ability to refuse him if he did not accede to her terms. Watching her with a strange, unreadable expression deep in the cool grey, that sent a tingle down the length of Rane's spine.

'Is it a bargain or not?' The tingle threatened to become a tremble, and Rane pressed him urgently for an answer before it undermined her determination and her resolution failed, and the sole arrow in her quiver blunted before it had time to find its mark.

'Answer me. Answer....' her taut nerves begged silently, and after an interminable pause that Rane thought would never come to an end, Greville answered,

'I'll find the sketches for you,' he promised, with a confidence that gave Rane a moment of wonder, but it passed almost as soon as it began, and jubilation at her victory lit her eyes with triumph as she placed the gemstone on the dark, matt surface of the carpet, and turned her attention to her camera.

'Will you need lights?'

It was her turn now, as the expert, and she savoured it to the full, and answered him briskly,

'No, my camera's got an automatic flash.'

It lit the study, brighter than the diamond nestling in its cushion of rock. 'I'll take several shots from different angles, just to be sure.' He watched her as she took them, and even the discipline of her work could not eliminate her acute awareness of his eyes following her every movement, tensing the muscles at the back of her neck until she feared the tension might react on her forearms and hands, resulting in camera shake and ruined photographs.

'It'll make a huge solitaire, or whatever.' Thankfully Rane took the final shot and raised herself up from her knees.

'The stone won't be used whole,' Greville laughed outright. 'It'd be much too ungainly. It'll be cut in half, and faceted into two cut stones. The octahedron shape,' he traced it with a sensitive forefinger, 'is usual for a diamond crystal, and it lends itself easily to being cut to make two matching stones.'

'You'd better have it back, in case I decide to run away with it.' Rane handed it back, and Greville took it from her and remarked easily,

'Diamonds aren't your stone.' He returned it to the

safe, reversing his previous movements so that the picture swung back to its former position, and the room returned to normal. 'You should wear emeralds, to match the colour of your eyes.'

He turned from the safe and came towards her, palpitatingly close. Suddenly Rane's courage failed her. Desperately she wanted to run, but the study door was locked, denying her escape, and her feet seemed to be glued to the floor, refusing to move as Greville reached out a lazy hand and took her chin unhurriedly between forefinger and thumb, tilting her head back so that he could look down into her wide, startled eyes.

'They're green, and they sparkle.' She could not be sure whether he alluded to her eyes, or to emeralds, and she had not the breath with which to ask. It deserted her in a gasp as he lowered his head and slowly, tantalisingly, brushed his lips across her mouth.

'Always choose emeralds,' he advised her gravely.

'Lunch is served, Mr Greville.'

A discreet knock on the door, and the voice of the trim maid who brought him the copy of the *Echo*. Contrarily Rane felt thankful that the door *was* locked, and then Greville straightened up, his fingers left her chin and he answered,

'Thank you, Ellen, we're coming.'

The moment was past. Greville unlocked the door, and Rane preceded him towards the dining room in a daze, reluctant to allow food to bespoil her lips that pulsated still from Greville's fleeting kiss.

'I see you're back from your joyride,' Zilla remarked sourly as they sat down. The ride had brought Rane as much pain as joy, but Zilla was not to know that, and the venom in the mannequin's voice told Rane she would not easily forgive her for the carriage ride with Greville, even though it was not of her seeking. It tipped the scales of Zilla's jealousy, and made an enemy of the other girl, but at the moment Rane did not care. She was too engrossed with the turmoil of her own feelings to bother too much about Zilla's.

'Isn't Leo coming down to lunch?' Deftly she steered the conversation into what she hoped was a safer channel.

'Mr d'Arvel asked for a working lunch to be sent to his room, miss, so I took him up something on a tray,' the maid answered her question, and Zilla snapped,

'I suppose you're satisfied, now you've sidetracked Leo away from the only really good designs in his Autumn Collection. He could easily have done them again from memory.' It was a gross libel on Leo's other work, of which the Harvest Collection was only a part, and a hot retort bubbled to Rane's lips, but before she could speak Greville interrupted smoothly,

'The missing designs could still turn up, there's been no mention of them in this morning's edition of the *Echo*, and I imagine if your reporter had taken them, he wouldn't have passed by the opportunity to publish his find.'

Which meant Greville still doubted that the designs were genuinely missing. 'He probably thinks it was simply a red herring, thought up on the spur of the moment when he discovered me in Leo's bedroom,' Rane thought angrily, but she refused to allow herself to shout the angry denials that longed to burst from her lips, effectively wiping away the sweetness of his kiss, and leaving in its place the bitter taste of galled pride that would only be lowered still further if she allowed Zilla the satisfaction of witnessing an open quarrel between herself and Greville. With massive self-restraint Rane announced tightly,

'There's still the Summer Collection to finish photographing. I'll work indoors this afternoon.' She felt she had had enough of the outdoors for one day. 'I'll be ready in the drawing room in half an hour from now.'

On the stroke of two o'clock she collected her box of equipment from where she left it in the hall after the morning session, and wondered out loud if Zilla would turn up, or defect as she threatened to until Leo could be present. 'If she doesn't come, I'll collect the clothes to be photographed from Marie, and you can model them for me,' she told the unresponsive suit of armour with a quirk of humour that vanished as swiftly as it surfaced when Zilla joined her, and she saw what the mannequin was wearing.

'Shelley was supposed to model that suit,' she said bluntly. The sage green silk was at least a size too big for Zilla, and the slim-cut jacket and skirt hung on her too spare frame.

'Marie handed it out to me, so I put it on,' Zilla shrugged unhelpfully. 'And Shelley's not here,' she added indisputably, with a 'take it or leave it' air.

'If Marie gave it to you, Leo must want you to model it,' Rane frowned, and privately regretted her impulsive offer to Leo, that left her to cope alone with the mannequin's notoriously temperamental behaviour.

'I'll have to use clips on the jacket and the skirt,' she decided discontentedly. 'It's a pity, because I wanted a shot of this particular suit taken in front of that full-length mirror, which would have shown the front view and the detail on the back at the same time. Oh well,' she reached resignedly for the row of bulldog clips neatly laid out in her box of equipment, 'stand still, where I can see the front of the suit in the mirror, so that I can be sure to draw it in evenly.'

Somewhat to her surprise, Zilla did as she was told, and forbore to fidget as Rane took up the slack material in a row of tightly packed clips, until from the front view the suit looked to be a perfect fit.

'Which hat?' she enquired, standing back to criticise the effect.

'The green straw with the wide brim.'

It exactly matched the suit, and Zilla added a chunky white necklace and long white gloves, then struck a pose with her hands resting on the handle of a long green and black striped umbrella.

'Will this do?' The mannequin stared into the middle distance, the epitome of cool elegance.

'Super!' Professionalism overcame personal feelings, and thankful for the other woman's unexpected co-operation, Rane quickly took several shots from different angles, regretfully omitting the one in the mirror, which itself was an ornate antique of impressive proportions that made her determined to include it in at least one of her photographs before she left.

'That's the end of my film. Hang on for a few minutes while I remove it, then I'll take the clips off the suit for you.'

'Marie can take them off upstairs, I'm going to change and go out for a walk.'

No doubt Greville's announced intention at lunch-time to inspect the flock of sheep in the park, was the reason for Zilla's uncharacteristic urge to take exercise, Rane thought cynically.

'I shan't be more than a minute or two,' she expostulated out loud, but Zilla declined to wait.

'Get your clips back from Marie,' she flung over her shoulder as she made for the door.

'Of all the selfish, inconsiderate . . .!' Rane slipped out the used film and replaced it with a fresh one, trained by years of experience never to leave her camera unloaded in case an unexpected picture should present itself, and find her unready.

'It didn't take five minutes,' she fumed crossly, 'and now I've got to waste twice that amount of time going upstairs to Marie to retrieve my clips!'

Zilla herself could not have wasted a single second in changing. The mannequin was already on her way downstairs, dressed for the outdoors, when Rane reached the drawing room door, and vouchsafed never a glance in her direction as she hurried outside.

'Trying to catch up with Greville,' Rane muttered sourly, and trudged up the stairs with an ill grace to find Marie. She was halfway up when a high-pitched screech of fury located the elderly dresser for her, and sent Rane's feet on wings of fear up the last half dozen steps.

'Marie, what on earth's the matter?'

'*You* ask *me* what is the matter?' Marie stood in the doorway of the room and fairly bristled with temper, while Rane regarded her with open-mouthed astonishment. The elderly Frenchwoman had every Latin's capacity for spectacular displays of emotion, but it was obvious that she was deeply upset, and it was equally obvious that, whatever the cause, she blamed Rane for it.

'What's going on?' Leo had evidently heard the commotion in his room, and appeared on the landing with a sketchbook in one hand, and a pencil in the other.

'Search me,' Rane shrugged helplessly. 'I can't begin to think what's come over her.'

'Did you think, before you ruined this so-lovely suit with your great, clumsy clips?' Marie brandished the jacket in her hand. 'First you insist on photographing Zilla in a garment made for Shelley to model, then you destroy the suit on her back!'

'The clips won't hurt the suit, Marie. You must

have seen them used dozens of times before, when the mannequins are modelling garments that are too big for them. I'd have taken them off myself, but Zilla was in a hurry to get changed and go out.'

'I've seen them used before, *oui*, but like this—*nevair!*' Marie shrilled, her English disintegrating under the emotion of the moment. 'And as for taking them off, remove them yourself, if you can!' With an angry hand she raised the sage green jacket and flung it straight at Rane.

'Remove them, if you can!' she shouted, and stormed back into the room, slamming the door behind her with a bang that shook the house.

'I can't think what Marie's making all the fuss about.' One of the clips on the back of the jacket caught Rane a sharp knock on her hand, and she winced as she turned in exasperation to Leo. 'They're quite easy to open ... oh, my goodness, this one's stuck!' With rising agitation she struggled to prise open the first bulldog clip, but obdurately it refused to budge. She tried again, with another, and another, all with the same negative result.

'Let me try.' Leo's stronger fingers produced no better results, and he turned accusing eyes on Rane's dismayed face.

'Why have you done this to me, Rane?' he cried. 'First my designs went missing, and now this! The garment's a complete write-off,' he groaned.

'But I haven't done anything,' Rane stammered, her bewilderment increasing. 'They're the same clips that I've used dozens of times before.'

'Perhaps it's what you haven't done, that's caused the trouble.' Leo looked ready to weep. 'You should have checked that the clips were clean before you used them.'

'They're always clean,' Rane insisted. 'They're clipped on to rods covered with foam rubber, and they never leave my equipment box until I need to use them.'

'They weren't clean this time,' Leo assured her grimly, and handed her back the jacket so that she could see for herself. 'Something must have leaked in your equipment box. The gripping surfaces of the clips are covered with a clear glue of some kind, and its soaked into the silk of the suit and hardened like cement. It's impossible to remove the clips without tearing the material to shreds!' he wailed despairingly.

CHAPTER SEVEN

RANE viewed Shelley's arrival at the weekend with heartfelt relief.

Marion had remained in her room, using her cold as an excuse, but primarily, Rane suspected, sulking because Leo was too immersed in the work of his new designs to spend any time with her. Since the episode of the suit, Marie had exuded an air of angry disapproval towards Rane that effectively kept her at a distance, and Zilla refused point blank to model any more clothes until Leo was there to supervise the proceedings. On two consecutive days Greville disappeared after breakfast and remained away until dinner, and his uncommunicative attitude when he returned rebuffed any attempt to throw a light on what he might have been doing during the day, and Rane was left to her own resources to fill in the empty hours as best she might.

'Thank goodness you've come!' she greeted Shelley's return with an exuberance that raised a merry chuckle from the mannequin.

'Surely you're not tired of the fleshpots already?' she joked, and asked curiously, 'Where is everybody?'

'Ill, busy, or on strike,' Rane replied tersely, and poured out the happenings of the last few days into Shelley's receptive ears.

'What could have leaked in your equipment box, to make such a mess on your clips?' Shelley frowned at her news.

'There's nothing in my box that could possibly leak,' Rane retorted positively. 'I never print my own films, they're all done in the lab in London, so I've got no liquid of any kind among my bits and pieces, and certainly not glue.'

'Marie said there was glue on the clips.'

'The foam rubber that covers the rods where I keep the clips when they're not in use, was saturated with glue,' Rane confirmed gloomily. 'It soaked up the stuff like a sponge, and of course when I came to use the clips, the gripping surfaces were liberally coated. Nothing else in the box was touched by it.'

'It's a pity you had to choose that particular time to insist on Zilla modelling the silk suit,' Shelley remarked reproachfully. 'You wouldn't have needed to use the clips if I'd modelled it myself as planned, because it's in my size.'

'I didn't insist on Zilla modelling the suit. Whatever makes you think that?' Rane asked her with asperity. Marie had said much the same thing, but at the time she had put it down to the hysteria of the moment, and taken less notice of the elderly dresser's remark than she probably should have done. 'At the time, I questioned the fact that Zilla was wearing the suit instead of you, but she said Marie handed it out to her to put on, so I supposed Leo must have left instructions for Zilla to model it instead.'

'Zilla told Marie that *you* insisted upon her wearing it, for a special picture you wanted to take,' Shelley said slowly and significantly, and Rane stared at her for a long moment.

'You don't think that Zilla . . .?' she breathed at last. 'Oh, no, she wouldn't do such a thing—would she?' she appealed to Shelley.

'She would if she got half the chance.' The younger mannequin had no illusions about her colleague's potential. 'You know she's got a spiteful streak in her makeup.'

'Yes, but to deliberately ruin an exclusive model, and leave me to reap the blame. . . .' Such behaviour was outside Rane's ken, and the distress in her voice showed it. 'I've done nothing to warrant such treatment from Zilla,' she protested.

'You went for a ride in the carriage with Greville,' Shelley pointed out.

'That was Greville's doing, not mine.'

'So much the worse, from Zilla's point of view,' the mannequin retorted shrewdly. 'How long were you away?'

'Ten minutes . . . twenty. . . .' The minutes had been as long as an Arctic night, and as blissfully fleeting as a shooting star. 'I don't know,' Rane answered helplessly.

'Long enough for Zilla to pour glue over the foam rubber mounting for the clips into your equipment box, which you conveniently left unattended in the hall while you were away.'

'It's all conjecture,' Rane pointed out, 'I can't prove anything, and Zilla, if it was she who did it, isn't likely to own up. I'll just have to be extra careful from now on, that's all.' As if she was not already faced with enough difficulties, she would now have to mount guard over her own possessions, she realised bleakly.

'No, you can't prove anything,' Shelley admitted, 'but just the same I think Leo ought to be told.'

'I can't worry Leo,' Rane was adamant. 'He's got his work cut out to complete the wedding dress design, I won't have him disturbed with trivialities.'

'I'd argue with you about this being trivial,' Shelley countered, 'but you're quite right, Leo's more than got his work cut out to finish his design—he's decided to include the wedding dress in his Summer Collection. Marie told me.'

'*What?*' Rane's eyes widened. 'He'll never do it in

the time,' she exclaimed. 'After he's finished his sketches, there's all the work of making it up.'

'He'll do it, never fear,' Shelley laughed. 'He's working like a demon. According to Marie, he *is* a demon, to expect her to get his inspiration made up in time for the showing at the end of the month, to say nothing of photographing it here first. She's not only got to replace the silk suit that was ruined, she's now got to cope with the wedding dress and all that entails, and since apparently the suggestion for the bridal outfit came from you in the first place, she blames you for that, as well as the suit. I gather you're not exactly popular upstairs at the moment,' she twinkled.

'I suggested Greville's landau as the perfect background for a bridal dress,' Rane agreed, and added ruefully, 'If Greville has his way, Leo won't ever come to Fullcote Hall again, so he probably thinks this is his last chance to use the carriage, and he's not going to miss the opportunity.'

'More than likely,' Shelley agreed, 'but if you won't let Leo know what we suspect, I think you should mention it to Greville.'

'No!' Rane exploded forcefully. 'This is an internal matter between us, as Leo's team, it's none of Greville's business.'

'What, may I ask, is not my business?' Greville's voice enquired suavely from behind them, and both girls spun round.

'There's been sabotage,' Shelley began dramatically.

'It's an internal matter between Leo's team,' Rane intervened quickly, her tongue recovering more rapidly than her heartbeat, as that ill-used organ leapt erratically at the sound of the familiar tones, making her voice ragged as she added repressively, 'It's of neither interest nor concern to an outsider.'

'Everything that happens under my roof is of both

interest and concern to me,' Greville retorted crisply. There was steel in his voice, steel in the look that lanced across the intervening space between them, reminding her that it was Leo and his team, and not Greville, who were the outsiders at Fullcote Hall. 'Sabotage is a serious accusation to level at anybody,' he reminded her curtly.

'It couldn't have been you,' Shelley dispensed candid acquittal, 'you were taking Rane for a drive in the carriage when it happened. Sorry, Rane,' belatedly the mannequin became conscious of the victim's scarlet face and frantic signals for silence, 'but Greville's bound to hear about it sooner or later, so it's best to tell him the true version at source,' she said practically, and ignoring Rane's obvious discomfort, she proceeded to do so with irritating relish.

'Have you any idea who might be responsible?' Greville asked gravely when Shelley paused for breath, and Rane cut in quickly before the other girl could reply.

'None at all,' she lied robustly, and glared a warning to Shelley. If the other girl named Zilla as the suspect, Greville was bound to ask what reason the mannequin might have for doing such a thing, and Rane's cheeks gained an even deeper hue at the possibility that Shelley might blurt out what she suspected. 'I've absolutely no idea,' she stated firmly.

'Well, it couldn't have been Leo or Marie, and I've only just come, so I'm in the clear.' Adroitly Shelley sidestepped the issue, and promptly laid a glaring trail of clues that must have made it obvious to Greville who she meant. He would automatically exonerate his ward, which only left Zilla. Rane felt she could cheerfully smack Shelley, and before the other girl was tempted to enlarge she changed the subject with what she hoped was a convincing display of impatience.

'All this is getting us nowhere,' she snapped. 'The whole affair's wasted enough time as it is, and there's little enough left if Leo wants the wedding outfit included in the Summer Collection. I've still got the summer dress to photograph out of doors. I think I'll use the picnic scene as a background.' Cruelly she punished Shelley for her perfidy, driving her into the peach and white off-the-shoulder print that brought out goose pimples on her own flesh at the mere thought of braving the icy wind clad in such an inadequate gament. 'Afterwards I want to come back and take some shots of the various accessories. No, I won't want you for that,' conscience made her release Shelley. 'I can scatter them on a chair or something, and take them through the big mirror. It'll work up into a corner picture in case we need to fill a space in one of the pages.'

'You're a sadist,' Shelley acknowledged her punishment, but added accommodatingly, 'I'll go up and get changed right away, Marie's got everything ready, though if you've chosen a site too far away from the house, we'll have to use your car or mine to carry the props in.'

'We can manage a tartan rug and an empty picnic basket between us,' Rane decided. 'We'll set it up under the beech tree that stands on its own at the far end of the lake.'

'It's a goodish way to walk, lumbered with props,' Shelley grumbled, 'and don't forget you'll have to take along your equipment box as well. That isn't empty, and it's far from light to carry. From now on you'll have to take it with you everywhere you go, and keep an eye on it,' she reminded Rane.

'The Bentley's outside the door, why not use that?' Greville offered obligingly, and Rane opened her mouth to refuse, but he added quickly, 'Regard it as one of the props.' His glance levelled with her own, challenging her, daring her to refuse his offer. He had driven her into a corner, and he knew it. A beech tree and a lake could be sited in any public park, but the Bentley, showing discreetly to one side of her picture, would provide the up-market image Leo so desired, making it difficult—impossible—for Rane to say no, she realised furiously.

'Great! I can't miss the chance of another ride in the Bentley. Don't go without me, you two,' Shelley accepted for her, unhooking Rane from the horns of one dilemma, and promptly impaling her on the even sharper ones of another. Accepting the loan of the Bentley meant accepting Greville's presence at the modelling session, and Rane's already overstretched nerves quivered under the extra strain. She drew in a deep, unsteady breath. Perhaps the chauffeur. . . .

'I'll put this in the car for you, while we're waiting for Shelley.' Greville destroyed her frail hope before it was properly formed, scooped up the controversial equipment box in lean fingers, and made for the door. 'Oh, Ellen——' he paused and beckoned the young maid who was passing, and spoke briefly to her before resuming his errand, leaving Rane to stand frustrated and fuming on her own in the hall.

'Why didn't *you* keep an eye on my equipment box for me?' she vented her ruffled feelings on the innocent suit of armour. 'As a guard, you're just a useless piece of tin!' she slandered it unjustly.

'Talking to yourself?' Shelley teased, running downstairs clad in the obligatory ankle-length cloak over the summer dress, and burdened by a large wicker basket and a gay travel rug.

'Take a hold of one of these,' she dumped the rug in to Rane's arms and asked, 'Where's Greville gone?'

'He's here.' The object of her enquiry reappeared

through the door, and relieved both the girls of their respective burdens. 'Front seat or back?' he enquired of them as they reached the car.

'Back,' they both chorussed in unison, and he lifted a quizzical eyebrow.

'One in the back with the props, and the other in front with me,' he stated firmly.

'Bags I the back seat,' Shelley responded promptly. 'I rode in the front when you took me to the station, and I want to try them both,' engagingly she excused her preference.

'You're forgiven,' Greville laughed, and handed her into the desired seat and put the props in beside her.

'Your turn.' He held open the front passenger door, and Rane hesitated. The urge to turn her back on Greville and his Bentley, and travel on her own two feet instead, was almost irresistible.

'Hop in.' Impatience edged Greville's voice, demanding her instant compliance, and Rane's independent spirit revolted at his tone of command.

'I won't!' she began angrily, when Shelley wailed from the rear of the car.

'Hurry up, Rane, you're letting the wind into the car through that open door, and I'm freezing in this thin dress!'

'Don't spoil her pleasure in the ride.'

It was blackmail. Greville knew it, and Rane knew it, and there was nothing she could do about it. Maddeningly, Greville had won. Again. With set lips, Rane capitulated, averting her face so that she should not look at him, should not see the victory reflected in his lean features. She turned abruptly and scrambled into the front passenger seat, regretting that her slight build did not allow her to make the dignified entry that she was certain Zilla would have managed under the circumstances.

'Will this do?' Greville brought the Bentley to a halt near the edge of the lake, in just the right spot, Rane realised with unjustified irritation, to show in the background of her photographs without being unnecessarily intrusive. The discreet hint of opulence which was just what Leo wanted. . . .

'It'll do for the moment,' she replied ungraciously, and waited with ill-concealed impatience for Greville to release the door, determined not to repeat her former undignified struggle to open it before he released the automatic lock.

'Where do you want to spread the rug?' he asked when they foregathered on the turf.

'On the lake side of the tree.' The moment the words were out, Rane regretted them. 'I'll set up the props myself,' she declared crushingly. She was in charge of the photography session, and since she was obliged to accept Greville as an onlooker, she was determined he would remain that, and nothing more.

'This should be about right, I think.' He either did not hear her, or chose to ignore her last remark—more likely the latter, Rane told herself furiously, and with an ease aided by his impressive height he shook out the large rug, and with a quick glance at the available possibilities, laid it flat in exactly the place Rane herself would have chosen. She viewed the result discontentedly, wishing in vain that there was another such ideal spot for her purpose. There was none. She wished she had not taken out her ire on the hapless Shelley, and opted for an indoor photography session instead. It was too late.

'Perhaps I'll try the shots from the other side of the tree,' she hedged.

'If you shoot them from the other side, you'll get the daffodils in your picture,' Greville pointed out with infuriating accuracy.

'You mustn't take a picture of the daffs,' Shelley objected, 'it's supposed to be a summer scene. And you can't possibly pick all that lot out of the way,' she waved an airy hand at the great drifts of gold that clothed the grass on the far side of the beech.

'Let's spread the picnic things on the rug.' Rane hid her vexation in feverish activity, opening the basket and scattering the contents haphazardly about the rug.

'It's a good job the props aren't real china,' Shelley observed drily, 'that's the third one you've dropped.'

'My fingers are cold,' Rane snapped crossly. Her fingers were paralysed with nerves, not cold, numb with a tense awareness of Greville's eyes following her every movement. Irritably she wished he would go away, but instead he sat down comfortably on an exposed tree root, out of range of her camera, and seemingly impervious to the biting wind. Abruptly Rane turned her back on him, but she could not shut out her own acute awareness of his presence behind her. It penetrated the barricades of her consciousness, made her fingers clumsy, and atrophied her brain, so that when Shelley asked,

'Where do you want me to sit?' she replied distractedly,

'Oh, anywhere. Choose your own spot.' And she could have screamed aloud with frustration when Shelley chose the wrong spot, but with set lips she refused to retract, and grimly forced her finger to the shutter and her eye to the view-finder, that saw not the posing Shelley, but only Greville ... Greville ... Greville ...

'The swans think it's a real picnic, they're coming to the bank to beg for titbits.' Greville spoke, and Rane jumped nervously, blessing the fact that her camera was hung round her neck by a sturdy strap that prevented it from dropping out of her nerveless hands and ending its useful life on the turf at her feet.

'What a shame!' Shelley's sympathetic nature made her forget the Arctic conditions, and her own flimsy attire. 'I've got nothing to give to them.'

'There's some bread in the car.' Greville rose to his feet and strolled to the Bentley, returning with a small bread roll in his fingers. 'Give this to them,' he offered it to Shelley.

'Give it to them yourself!' Rane stormed angrily. 'Shelley's working,' she pointed out bluntly, 'she hasn't the time to feed swans. Besides, she mustn't risk marking the dress.'

'She could feed the swans and show off the dress at the same time,' Greville replied evenly, and deliberately gave the bread roll into Shelley's hands, and Rane drew in a tight breath with an outraged hiss that resembled that of the swans, at the audacity of his move.

'Where Shelley poses for the photographs is for me to decide,' she claimed furiously.

'It would make a lovely picture, Rane, and the bread roll isn't buttered, so it can't possibly mark the dress.' To Rane's chagrin the mannequin sided with Greville. 'If I pose like this, look, it'd be worth you taking a couple of trial shots, surely?' She ran lightly down to the water's edge, her hands outstretched with her offering, and instantly the two swans glided in close to the edge of the bank to investigate. It was a delightful picture, a scene straight from the ballet. The mannequin's arms stretched gracefully to meet the long white arched necks of the cob and pen, the back of her shoulders and neck rose bare and lovely from the low, scooped neckline of the peach and white print, and the clear water of the lake showed a perfect reflection of the front of the dress that was better than in any mirror. The skirt flowed outwards in a delicate

fan upon the rich green turf, and the steel grey of the
Bentley provided a stark contrast to one side. The
scene was bathed in bright sunshine, and breathed the
very essence of a summer's day.

'Take your picture quickly, before the swans move.'

Once again Greville took command, and once again,
against her will, Rane obeyed him. It was a unique
picture that would not present itself twice, and she
owed an obligation to Leo, and to the magazine that
employed her. Bitterly she repaid her obligations, in
suppressed anger and injured pride. Uncharitably she
wished Shelley would lose her balance and tumble into
the lake with the swans, and that Greville and his
Bentley would follow her.

'It'll make a superb picture, you won't regret taking
it.'

He was too late, she already did regret it—not only
the photograph, but the whole heart-destroying
business of being with Greville, under Greville's roof,
being forced to see him and talk to him while at the
same time keeping her true feelings for him ruthlessly
hidden behind a rigid barrier of self-control that, she
felt despairingly, was rapidly beginning to crack.

'I've taken enough pictures of this dress.' The end
of another clip of film gave her the excuse she needed
to cease operations, and this time, luckily, Shelley
made no demur.

'Thank goodness!' The mannequin shivered her
way back into the warm cocoon of her cloak, and
picked up her voluminous handbag.

'There's some hot coffee in the car,' Greville
offered, but Shelley shook her head.

'I daren't,' she murmured, 'it'd be just my luck to
have a spill, and one spoiled outfit in the Summer
Collection is quite enough. Marie would never survive
having to remake another model. In any case, she

wants me back as soon as possible to alter the hemline of the dress. Leo and his hemlines!' She raised her eyes heavenwards.

'In that case, I'll run you back to the house.'

'There's no need, I can see a Range Rover coming along the drive, I'll beg a lift in that.' Blithely Shelley thumbed the approaching vehicle, and turned to Rane as it swung across the turf towards them. 'I nearly forgot,' she dived into the depths of her handbag, 'I called in at your office on my way here this morning to see if there was anything for you, and Clive Redman asked me to give you this packet. He said they were photographs. Oh, Jack,' she broke off as the Range Rover drew to a halt beside them, and the groom popped an enquiring face through his driving window, 'will you give me a lift back to the house?' she smiled sweetly.

'That I will, miss,' the man assured her with alacrity. 'Jump in, it's warm in the cab.'

'Take the props back with you at the same time,' Greville instructed him, and Rane caught her breath. With Shelley gone, she would be left alone with Greville.

'Take me along, too,' she began urgently, but Jack had his back towards her, collecting the props, and did not appear to hear her, and Greville put a detaining hand on her arm and said,

'You can't let the coffee go to waste, and besides, I'm interested to see the photographs your editor sent to you. Some of them might be for me?' He referred obliquely to the photographs she had taken of the diamond.

'See you later,' Shelley called as Jack returned with the props to the Range Rover, and they pulled away, back on to the park road, and left Rane standing uncertainly beside Greville, her hands clutching her

camera and the packet of photographs, and panic
clutching at her heart as he said,

'Let's get into the back of the car where it's warm,'
and steered her dragging feet towards the Bentley.
Even the swans had deserted her, she saw bleakly. The
bread roll demolished, the two birds were now twin
white blobs sailing majestically in the middle of the
lake.

'This will thaw you out.' Nothing would thaw the
ice round her heart, but she circled her hands round the
beaker of coffee nevertheless. The scalding heat of it
burned her palms, but she refused to slacken her grip,
grasping at the pain of it to distract her mind from
the leaden pain that lay inside her breast, that no antidote could remove and no warmth could soothe away.

'Jack's left the props hamper in the car,' she
observed dully.

'It isn't the props hamper, it's mine. And what's
more, it's full of lunch.' Greville opened the lid to
show her. 'I thought we'd escape the atmosphere of
the dining room for one day,' he twinkled, and Rane
stared at him in astonishment.

'I didn't think you'd noticed,' she blurted out
unguardedly.

'Who could help but notice Leo, agonising over his
hemlines; Marion, sulking over Leo's neglect, and
Marie, muttering Latin imprecations about being
overworked,' Greville grinned. 'Let's play truant for
once, and enjoy our lunch by the lake,' he coaxed
persuasively, and grinned across at her with a
conspiratorial, schoolboy grin that transformed his
face. Rane watched him, fascinated. He had not
mentioned Zilla, and suddenly, happily, she did not
want to remind him. A bubble of gaiety rose inside her
to match his mood, sweeping away her black
despondency, and when Greville said, 'You must be

hungry,' she replied gaily, 'I'm starving!' and meant it.

Ellen had packed the hamper with small yeasty cobs, oven-baked and crusty, and still warm. Sharp cheese, and tiny fingers of sausage, and scones oozing with butter and strawberry jam, and they licked their fingers clean of the sticky sweetness of it like two children at a stolen feast, then shared the remains of the coffee. It was food for the gods, and the gods smiled upon them as they ate, tempting them to enjoy the enchanted moments to the full; no matter that outside the car blew the bitter wind of reality, inside there was only warmth, and sunshine, and each other.

'Your lips taste of strawberry jam.' He did not seem to mind the taste. Suddenly the hamper was swept out of the way, and Rane was in his arms, the food and drink forgotten. He bent his dark head close above her, and for a timeless moment his mouth clung to her own, lingering on her softly parted lips, exploring their tremulous fullness, until, with a long sigh, she relaxed in his arms, her antagonism forgotten, and her face lifted submissively to meet the masterful pressure of his kiss.

'Don't let's go back to the house yet,' Greville's voice sounded hoarse. 'Let's walk in the park for a while. I'll pick some daffodils for you.'

'The wind's keen.' Perhaps his hoarseness was the forewarning of a cold?

'The beeches will shelter us from the wind.'

'My equipment box. . . .'

'It'll be safe enough in the car. I'll lock the doors, so that nobody can get in.'

He overrode her objections, drawing her out of the car on to the emerald turf, while the lark rose again and trilled above them. Greville took her by the hand and ran her, laughing with him, until she was knee deep in daffodils, and her heart soared to join the small brown songster and carolled a duet with it to the beauty of the day.

'Pick the buds, they last longer.'

'Have some of the open ones as well, for colour in the meantime.'

He picked daffodils with extravagant abandon, a handful, an armful, that made not a jot of difference to the dancing drifts of gold that coloured the grass like sheets of sunshine under the mighty trees.

'Let me carry them,' Rane begged, and held out her arms.

'The stems are dripping sap.' He looked doubtful. 'It'll spoil your clothes.'

'I've only got on my old duffle coat and working slacks, and they don't matter.' She wanted to hold his daffodils, she needed to hold them, her first gift, perhaps the only one she would ever have, from Greville. Her eyes shone as he dropped them into her arms, and she buried her face in the gold, inhaling their fulsome earthy smell, redolent of the newly awakened spring.

'Wrap this round the end of the stems, it'll save your clothes a bit.' Greville reached up to his top pocket and shook out a neatly folded silk handkerchief, holding it out to her.

'I can't possibly use that,' she protested, 'it probably cost more than my duffle coat and slacks put together! I know,' she had an inspiration, 'I'll use the wrapping paper from round the parcel of photographs Clive sent to me. I put it in one of my coat pockets.' She delved deep into the capacious patch pockets of her duffle coat and came up with her editor's parcel, fumbling one-handed with the neatly taped wrapping, refusing to relinquish her daffodils in order to use both hands.

'Let me do it for you.' Greville took the parcel from her and slit open the wrapping with dexterous fingers, and extracting the folder that revealed itself inside, he shook out the sheet of brown paper, and gave it to Rane.

'That'll keep your flowers nicely bunched until we get back to the house.' He helped her to roll it round the fresh green stems to make a neat holder.

'Would you like this back in your pocket?' Punctiliously Greville resisted the temptation to have a look at the contents of the folder, and offered it back to Rane unopened.

'Let's go somewhere and look at the photographs together,' she suggested. Since Greville had been present at all the modelling sessions, there was no reason why he should not see the proofs, and with luck the pictures of his diamond would be included in their number as well. 'Shall we go back to the car? No, not the car,' she retracted hastily. If she suggested they return to the car, Greville might think she was trying to lure him into kissing her again. Her cheeks warmed at the thought. 'Let's stay with the daffodils,' she stammered instead, and hoped he would blame the deepened colour in her cheeks on the keenness of the wind.

'The beeches will give us shelter from the wind while we look at the photographs,' he said gravely, and Rane sent him a quick upwards glance from under her lashes, then dropped them again, confused by the twin devils of laughter that told her he had guessed the reason for her sudden change of mind, and derided her lack of courage, and suggested with suddenly narrowed lids that the beeches could provide just such a pleasant shelter as the car. . . .'

'The beeches. Yes, they'll do nicely,' she agreed raggedly. Scarlet flags of mortification stained her throat and cheeks to an even deeper hue, and she buried her face in her bouquet and wished she had accepted Greville's handkerchief to wind round the daffodil stems, or simply allowed the sap to soak into her coat.

'This tree root makes a handy seat.' He guided her to where the ancient beech lent its root to rest them, and the immense spreading girth of its bole to shelter them from the wind, turning the tiny glade into a warm suntrap that seemed destined just for the two of them.

'The swans have followed us.' She grasped thankfully at the diversion as the snowy pair cruised hopefully on the water a couple of feet away. 'We should have brought them something from the hamper,' she wished regretfully.

'There wasn't anything left,' Greville laughed, 'Ellen only packed lunch for two.'

It was as if the icy wind lanced right through the tree trunks at their backs, and pierced her heart.

'Lunch for two. . . .' Greville must mean himself and Shelley. He had brought along the hamper in the car, knowing the mannequin must feel bitterly cold after the photography session, in spite of her long cloak over the thin dress, not expecting her to refuse at least a coffee afterwards, for that reason. Expecting Rane to return to the house to take the desired photographs of the dress accessories through the mirror, leaving himself and Shelley alone in the car. Rane swallowed on a throat that hurt. She had eaten the food, and drunk the coffee, both of them intended for Shelley. In other words, she had been used as second best, because Shelley had refused them. Another possibility flashed unbidden across her mind, and she caught her breath on a hard note of pain. When Greville kissed her, had he used her as second best then, as well? The hectic flush drained from her cheeks and left them a ghastly white. Anger and humiliation burned in her at the way in which he had

used her, and she wanted to lash out and hurt him as
he had hurt her. She was barely conscious of his long
fingers riffling through the coloured proofs beside her,
the bright prints danced in front of her eyes,
unrecognisable through the mist of anger that clouded
her vision.

'This photograph of Marion in the cornflower blue
dress is lovely. I'd like a copy of that one, to keep for
myself,' Greville observed approvingly.

'Ask Leo for it,' Rane snapped back. 'He probably
won't want the proof, since he's got Marion herself,'
she added provokingly. Her barb found its mark, and
Greville's fingers stilled, and his face hardened, and
his voice cut with the chill of the wind as he retorted
harshly.

'On the contrary, Leo will need his photograph to
keep as a souvenir.'

He was so sure that his own wishes would prevail,
and that Leo would lose Marion. The arrogance of the
man! Rane's eyes flashed fire, and she longed to do
something, anything, to dent his sublime self-
confidence in his own essential rightness to dictate the
lives of other people.

'I'll take these photographs of the diamond.' He
fanned the last few proofs in his hand like a pack of
playing cards. 'They'll be adequate for identification
and insurance purposes.'

Adequate? The description was an insult to her
professional standards, and Rane's temper spilled over.

'I suppose you've got the future of your diamond all
neatly ordered and pigeonholed as well,' she bit
sarcastically. 'At least the gemstone can't argue about
its fate!'

'Quite right, it can't,' Greville's voice was clipped.
'I've got its destination all worked out,' he goaded her,
and waited, but with tight lips Rane refused to

respond to his bait and ask what its destination might
be, suddenly, chillingly afraid that the answer might
be, the third finger of Shelley's left hand, and if it was,
she could not bear it, she did not want to know. She
moved, a sudden, convulsive drawing away from the
pain of knowing, and Greville spoke sharply.

'Mind the photographs . . . your flowers!'

The end of her bunch of daffodils caught the fan of
proofs in his hand, the brown paper wrapping making
a rigid parcel that gave the thin paper squares a blow
that sent them spinning from Greville's hand and
scattered them face upwards on the grass at their feet.

'It's a good job the grass is dry,' Greville growled.

'They're perfectly all right, there's not a mark on
them,' Rane retorted defensively—and then stopped.
'Face upwards' was an apt description of the one proof.
She stared down at it, in total dismay, and Greville's
likeness stared back at her from the grass, angry,
accusing, the face of the stranger caught in her camera
lens in the Paris fashion salon, it seemed a lifetime ago.
The stranger who was not a stranger any more, but who
sat beside her on the tree root, and seemed more of an
enigma now than he had been when she took the
photograph. What was it doing, among the rest of the
photographs in the packet? she wondered bewilderdly.

'Your editor's pinned a note to this one for you.'
Greville leaned down and retrieved the picture of
himself, and his eyes flicked over the note pinned on
to it, written in Clive Redman's unmistakable bold,
black script. It said,

'Found your pin-up in the bottom drawer of your
desk. Hope he lives up to expectations, now you know
him better.'

Curse Clive, for his habit of rummaging in her desk
for anything from a rubber band to biscuits for his
elevenses! Scarlet with mortification, Rane poured

silent maledictions on her absent editor's head, for his ill-timed sense of humour. He could hardly have chosen a worse time to return the photograph to her, if he had tried.

'Found your pin-up. . . .' She ground her teeth in helpless rage at the inference. Nothing could be more calculated to feed Greville's ego than this, she thought furiously. He could not help but read the note Clive had written, the bold, black strokes stood out like poster paint. How Greville must be laughing at her! First he duped her into responding to his kisses, using her as a substitute for Shelley, and then he discovered she had kept his photograph in her desk. He probably thinks I've been yearning over it like a lovesick teenager, she told herself wretchedly, and winced away from how near the truth that was.

'I'll take these in and give them to Leo.' Shakily she bent to scoop up the shots of the mannequins, using the move to hide her scarlet face as she jumbled the proofs together in her hands, careless of whether they were the right way up or not.

'Put this one with them.' Greville held it out to her, his eyes probing her face, waiting for her to take the print from his hand. 'You'll want it. . . .'

'Keep the photograph, I don't want it.' Rane jerked away from the photograph as if it might bite. 'I don't want it, I tell you! Nor your daffodils,' she cried shrilly as he continued to hold out the print towards her, his expression inflexible, determined to make her take it back. 'I don't keep souvenirs,' she cried, and jumped to her feet, spilling her armful of daffodils. The brown paper wrapping burst open and scattered the blooms over the grass, over Greville. Instinctively he grabbed at them to save them, and the photograph flew from his hand.

'Be careful. . . .' She did not want the photograph,

and she could not let it go. She snatched at the paper as it flew past her, but the wind got there first, and with a mischievous puff it flipped the proof towards the lake, and without pausing to think Rane ran after it, sending the swans paddling in alarm away from their station close to the bank. With flailing hands she reached up to snatch at it as it hovered over the water, but the wind only laughed, and tossed the photograph higher, taking it in the wake of the swans.

'Be careful, you'll fall in!'

Greville shouted, then Rane's feet slipped, and she forgot the photograph in a desperate fight to keep her balance as the edge of the bank crumbled beneath her feet and tipped her sideways towards the lake.

'Another second, and you'd have been wet through.' Greville caught her with hard hands and pulled her unceremoniously on to terra firma, and demanded angrily, 'Do you think a photograph's worth risking pneumonia for?'

It lay face upwards, bobbing up and down on the eddies left by the departing swans, slowly sinking below the surface even as she watched it, the features becoming blurred as it sank lower and lower into the water. It was like an indictment on her earlier wish that Greville and his Bentley might fall into the lake. Rane's overwrought nerves recoiled from the simile, and a sob broke from her lips as the saturated photograph finally buckled and sank out of sight, and she rounded on Greville and shouted hysterically,

'No, I don't think the photograph's worth it! And neither is the original!'

With the strength of desperation she twisted herself free from his grip and flung away from him, stumbling blindly across the grass towards the house, scarcely able to discern the building for the scalding tears that made her cheeks as wet as the lost photograph.

CHAPTER EIGHT

'HAPPY birthday, Marion!'

'Happy birthday!'

The chorus of good wishes was superfluous. Marion exuded happiness. Her step was light, and her face glowed. She had the look of nineteen years old, with the world at her feet. She had the look, Rane thought with a quick pang of envy, of someone who has just been soundly kissed by the man she loved. She danced rather than walked into the breakfast room, swinging hands with Leo, and his face, too, reflected the same brightness that had been markedly lacking in both of them for the past few days. Rane soon discovered the cause.

'Leo's finished his design of the wedding dress, and he's not going to do any more work until tomorrow,' Marion smiled. 'We can have the whole of my birthday together,' she gloated happily.

'When Leo's pencil stops work, my scissors have to start,' Marie complained to the room at large. The gloom had left the faces of the young couple and settled on that of the elderly Frenchwoman instead.

'I'll have to work as well,' Shelley pointed out cheerfully. 'We haven't got a wooden dummy here to fit the toile on, so you'll have to use me to model it for you instead.' She turned to Rane. 'A toile's a sort of trial run of a design, made up in white canvas,' she explained. 'It allows any mistakes to be ironed out and alterations to be made before the design's made up in the final material. But we've got Marion's party to look forward to this evening,' she comforted Marie.

'It's all very well for you,' the disgruntled Frenchwoman refused to be appeased. 'You don't have to work your fingers to the bone, like me. What with another suit to make,' she sent a barbed look in Rane's direction, 'and now the wedding dress as well! You go away when the day's modelling's finished, I have to stay here and continue to work!'

'On the contrary,' Shelley contradicted her blithely, 'Greville's asked me to stay for the rest of the weekend, so I'll be here to help you.'

'Greville's asked me to stay. . . .' Rane's heart descended to her shoes, and her spirits followed suit. So Greville *was* in love with Shelley. Her intuition had been devastatingly accurate. Why else would Greville ask Shelley to remain at Fullcote Hall over the weekend? True, he had extended the same invitation to Zilla, but only because the older mannequin tricked him into it. With Shelley it was different. She would scorn to use tricks, so the invitation must be a genuine one, extended because Greville himself wanted her to stay.

Painfully, all sorts of pointers presented themselves to Rane's tortured mind, small things that had not been apparent to her at the time but which seemed glaringly obvious now. The way in which Greville had sought out Shelley to talk to on the first day she came to join in the modelling sessions. The alacrity with which he had offered his Bentley to take her back to the station when she returned to town, driving the car himself instead of sending it with his chauffeur. Using the car again to drive down to the lake yesterday afternoon, and taking hot coffee as an inducement to entice the frozen mannequin back to the warmth of the car afterwards. Back to the warmth of his embrace. Rane closed her eyes against the agonising memory of it.

'Does my ring dazzle you? I'm not surprised,' Marion spoke gaily from beside her, and held out her right hand for Rane to see. 'It's lovely, isn't it? Greville gave it to me this morning.'

Perforce Rane had to open her eyes. The sapphire and diamond dress ring adorning the girl's finger was indeed very lovely. It was also, even to Rane's untutored eyes, very, very valuable. She risked a glance at Leo's face. The young designer was regarding his beloved's ring with marked lack of enthusiasm.

'It probably eclipses anything he can afford at the moment for her engagement ring,' Rane guessed intuitively, and felt swift anger rise in her at Greville's choice of a gift.

'It isn't a gift,' she told herself hotly, 'it's a weapon, aimed at Leo.' And from the expression on the young Frenchman's face, it had found its mark very successfully. Cruelly, it contrasted the difference in Marion's present life style with what she could expect if she left it and married the up-and-coming young designer. Rane's eyes left Leo's face and found Greville's on the other side of the room, attracted as if by a magnet to meet his cool grey stare that rested on her face, she realised with sudden unease, as if he had been watching her, gauging her own reaction to the ring, as well as Leo's.

'I hate you for doing this.' She did not attempt to hide her reaction. Her eyes flashed the message across to him, condemning him for his action. 'It's despicable! Unspeakable!' And her anger was akin to hurling gravel at a granite wall, she realised irefully. His cool eyes read her message, understood it, and tossed it indifferently back to her, rejecting her condemnation because its source meant less than nothing to him. Rane clenched her fists until her nails dug excruciatingly into her palms, and from what seemed a long way away she became aware of Marion asking her,

'Do you like my ring, Rane?'

'Yes. Yes, of course I like it. It's beautiful.' With an effort she wrenched her eyes away from Greville, and forced them to look again at the ring, trying to mask her dislike of the jewel and its donor that must have matched Leo's for ferocity.

'It's beautiful!' Marion obviously thought so, although her delight in the gift did not entirely account for the glow that lit the girl's face like a candle, and Rane wondered uneasily what lay behind her sudden joie de vivre. An underlying excitement brought a sparkle to Marion's eyes and a glow to her cheeks, that augured something more than birthday high spirits. Perhaps it was simply the prospect of a whole day spent in Leo's company. Perhaps it was the wedding dress, which she must know he had designed with herself in mind? Or perhaps they had become secretly engaged. Rane sent the couple a searching look. Were they planning to defy Greville's wishes? she wondered uneasily. Perhaps even elope?

'Don't do it, Marion,' Rane found herself begging silently, and wondered at herself even as the warning flashed across her mind. Surely she should be encouraging the young couple, rather than the other way around? She was on Marion's side, not Greville's. . . .

'When can I borrow you, to take your birthday photograph?' With an effort she pulled her thoughts back to her surroundings and forced herself to speak lightly, and Marion responded with a laugh.

'Not today, that belongs to Leo. Say tomorrow morning, and we'll both come and be photographed together?' she suggested, and unconsciously Rane relaxed. If the two were planning to elope, it was not to be tonight.

'Won't you be tired after your party?' she teased. 'I don't want my modest birthday present to be spoiled by dark rings under your eyes.'

'We shan't be staying up late tonight, it's only a token party because it's my birthday,' Marion assured her. 'I'm having my real party in Paris, after the showing of Leo's Collection.'

Would the party in Paris be a late birthday celebration, or a secret wedding reception? Rane wondered silently, but aloud she promised,

'I'll present you with a cabinet-sized photograph of both of you together, in a frame of your choice,' and wondered if Marion would be at Fullcote Hall to receive her gift when it was ready, or whether it would end up in Greville's possession, as an unwanted souvenir such as he had wished on Leo.

She was still turning the possibility over in her mind when she went upstairs to change for dinner that evening. In spite of the fact that it was the weekend, the day had been a busy one, the work mostly of her own making, done indoors in order to avoid bumping into Greville. She involved Shelley without conscience, taking advantage of the mannequin's presence to photograph several outfits that could have waited until after the weekend, and should have been modelled by Zilla, to the latter's intense annoyance, made the more acute when Marie claimed her services upstairs in lieu of Shelley.

'It's Zilla's own fault,' Rane excused herself, 'she won't model anything unless Leo's present, and since he's gone missing with Marion. . . .'

'Good for Leo!' Shelley grinned, and obligingly posed in outfits suitable for morning, afternoon, and after dark with a cheerful co-operation that disposed of the work in half the time that it would have taken with Zilla. Lunch was brief, and buffet, and Rane manoeuvred the work to make herself and Shelley so late that Greville had finished his meal and gone by the time they reached the dining room.

'That only leaves the sage green silk to photograph when it's been remade, and then the wedding dress,' Rane observed at last, with a satisfaction that was tempered by the realisation that, once the last two models had been photographed, her stay at Fullcote Hall would be at an end.

'Marie told me the silk suit will be ready tomorrow morning,' Shelley offered. 'By working flat out, she should have the toile of the wedding dress ready in twenty-four hours, and the model finished in the final material soon afterwards.'

'It'll have to be ready by Thursday morning at the latest, to meet my copy deadline, if Leo wants it to be included among the other photographs in the next issue of *Dress*,' Rane stated positively.

'It'll have to be packed up and back in Paris by Friday,' Shelley capped her timing. 'The showing of the Summer Collection is next Saturday,' she pointed out.

In a week's time all this would be nothing more than a memory. She would not even have Greville's photograph, to keep as a souvenir. Rane's feet dragged as they carried her upstairs to change, unlightened even by the prospect of wearing her new dress. She had packed it on impulse, unsure whether it would be called into use in her role as a working guest. It was in clear green taffeta, shot with gold, the colouring of the daffodils blowing in the parkland outside. The colouring of the daffodils that spilled sunshine into every corner of her bedroom.

Rane opened the door and stared at them in

astonishment. The golden blooms brightened the top of the dressing table; the small cabinet beside her bed; the polished floor in the far corner of the room, and the occasional table in the centre. An armful of blooms—Greville's blooms. Greville's clear answer to her saying she did not want them. She shut the door behind her, slowly, and leaned against it, staring at the blooms, and felt herself begin to tremble. Nothing she did, or said, could get the better of this man. The daffodils stared unwinkingly back at her, the golden trumpets like silent emissaries, witnessing her defeat. Rane sucked in a difficult breath and exploded away from the bedroom door, rage at his high-handed action taking her by the throat.

'I said I wouldn't have your flowers,' she choked, 'and I won't . . . I won't . . . I won't. . . .' With shaking hands she reached out to the bedside cabinet and snatched the flowers from their vase. Her fingers curled convulsively round the slender green stems, making their sappy freshness squeak with the force of her grip. 'I won't!' she sobbed, and pulled the blooms violently from out of their vase, heedless of their dripping stems.

'Bother!' The eternal housewife that resides in every woman checked at the wet stain that spread rapidly across a double sheet of white paper lying folded on the cabinet top, blotting paper that absorbed the water like a dark stain, running across it to join up with another dark stain already blotching the surface. Greville must have spilled the water, too, when he put the flowers in the vases, probably in haste in case she returned to her room and spoiled his element of surprise. The thought that she had forced him to hurry, and to spill the water, gave Rane a feeling of immense satisfaction.

'What a mess!' The blotting paper absorbed all the

water it was capable of taking, and a small pool began to form in its middle and started to run towards the edge, threatening the polished cabinet top.

'Oh, go back in your vase!' Impatiently Rane dumped the daffodils back in their receptacle, and grasped at the saturated blotting paper, lifting it hurriedly to try to prevent a spill. Her move proved too much for the beleaguered top fold, which promptly parted company with its bottom half and left Rane's fingers holding a piece of limp wetness, while her eyes stared in disbelief at the thing that lay revealed underneath.

The face of the stranger!

The photograph which she had last seen disappearing under water at the margin of the lake. Greville's face stared back at her, still easily recognisable on the now dry print, the satirical upward tilt of his well-cut lips scorning her opinion of his actions, as he had scorned it in the Paris fashion salon, taunting her futile attempts to prevail against his will.

'Keep your photograph. . . .' But he had retrieved it, and returned it to her, and the armful of daffodils as well, and with a deepening sense of despair Rane knew she would keep the photograph this time, as Greville intended she should. But to keep it did not necessarily mean she had to look at it.

'Where's your pride?' she stormed at herself angrily, and knew that it was gone as she picked up the print and dropped it face downwards into her suitcase, then slammed the lid, but still seeing every tiny feature of the pictured face clearly etched in lines of fire on her shrinking heart.

'Shall we dance?'

Dinner was over, the carpet was rolled back, and a Strauss waltz played invitingly on the stereo, and Greville, as befitted the perfect host, moved among his guests, dancing with each of the ladies in turn. He opened the dancing with Marion.

'He shouldn't have taken the first dance,' Rane criticised, 'that belongs to Leo.' But he took it nevertheless, and it was done and irreparable, then he danced with Shelley and Zilla, and now it was Rane's turn.

Panic shook her as he aproached across the floor. She gripped the arms of her chair until her knuckles turned white, longing to run from the room, anywhere so long as she did not have to give herself into Greville's arms and force her reluctant feet to step in time with his to the gay lilt of the dance, that to her strained nerves sounded more like the notes of a dirge.

'Shall we dance?'

Her legs refused to hold her, her feet refused to run, and there was no escape from Greville's arms. Mesmerised, Rane watched him come closer. Her throat felt dry and her palms felt clammy, and she wondered how she would manage to stand, let alone to dance.

'Did you find your daffodils?' He stood over her, looking down at her, and to anyone listening it must have sounded like the polite enquiry of a considerate host, making sure she had enough flowers in her room. Rane knew differently.

'Yes, I found them.' To her the daffodils were a banner, fluttering over the battle of wills that raged between herself and Greville, and in which so far she had been outclassed, outflanked, and out-manoeuvred. And now Greville had come to gloat over his latest victory.

'Yes, I found them.'

Quick temper sent a surge of new strength through her legs and turned the dirge into a rallying trumpet call, and as Greville's hand reached down to draw her to her feet, Rane rose swiftly, unaided, steeling herself against his touch.

'I won't mention the photograph,' she voted fiercely. 'I won't give him the satisfaction. . . .' The knowledge of the photograph lay like a no-man's-land between them, mined with pitfalls, a silent, waiting threat.

'The flowers won't last long, in the warmth of the house.'

'The buds will last.'

She had asked him to pick buds, for that very reason.

'I suppose so.' She forced her voice to indifference. The daffodil buds would last longer than the bud of her newly awakened love, that was doomed to wither before it had time to flower, for lack of reciprocal warmth to draw it forth into its full colour and beauty; they would last longer than the speeding hours, which would soon be passed and gone, and separate herself and Greville for ever.

'Tonight's the night, there'll be no more. . . .' The record changed, and a woman's voice echoed her thoughts with piercing accuracy, and Rane quivered as the words penetrated her raw nerves like a probe. She followed Greville's lead like an automaton as he swept her on to the floor. Like everything else he did, he danced superbly, and Rane's own inherent grace in the art followed his steps without effort, bound by the magic of the music to a oneness in the dance.

'Tonight's the night, there'll be no more. . . .'

She would not be present at Marion's birthday party in Paris. Once the last of the photographs was taken at Fullcote Hall, her work would be finished, and there would be no necessity for her to attend the showing of the Summer Collection at the salon. The desolation of the prospect drove a wedge of uncertainty between herself and her anger, and melted her resolution like snow before a south-blowing wind.

'Tonight's the night,' warned the singer throatily.

'Enjoy it while it lasts,' pleaded her heart piteously, and torn between the two, Rane's battle-weary spirit gave way.

'Just for tonight.' She hauled down her proud banner, dared the no-man's-land, and left her feet to avoid the pitfalls as best they could.

'Just for tonight,' she excused her capitulation. One perfect night out of a lifetime, and she would need the rest of that to contain her tears.

'You dance beautifully,' Greville murmured to the top of her head. Conventional words. Insincere words, but Rane tilted her head back and smiled up at him, her eyes thanking him for the words because they fitted the image of her perfect night.

'It's easy with a good partner,' she made the conventional reply, hardly conscious of speaking out loud, acutely conscious of Greville's hand holding her own, his slim fingers gripping hers easily, not too tightly, while his other hand pressed her lissom lightness close against him, holding her so that their steps merged and their bodies moved as one. So close that she could feel the deep vibration of his voice rumble through his broad chest when he spoke, and she leaned her head against it so that she could be even closer, closing her eyes and giving herself up to the heady intoxication of the moment.

'Just for tonight.'

It was a deadly intoxication, that would bring an aftermath of misery when the moment was passed, but like all such brews, while Rane quaffed deep of its sweetness she did not care.

'A toast to Marion.'

Rane emerged from a daze to find the music

stopped, a glass in her hand, and Greville beside her, proposing a toast,

'To Marion.'

The champagne bubbles stung her nose and sent their effervescence singing through her veins, inducing a lightheadedness that found no food to counteract its potency, since anger against Greville had closed her throat against her dinner.

'To Marion,' Rane echoed.

She tilted her glass, and with the courage gained from the champagne she added defiantly, in clear, ringing tones,

'And Leo.'

She felt Greville stiffen beside her, felt anger surge through him at her rash, public championship of the young couple. She did not look at him. She did not dare. To the room at large she might have been toasting Leo's success with his Summer Collection, but Greville knew her toast for what it was, and his anger sprang out against her, battering at her like a physical force, and she took another hasty gulp from the glass to bolster her courage that disconcertingly began to wane.

'To Marion and Leo.' The other guests took up her toast with enthusiasm, everyone, that was, except Greville. There was laughter and congratulations, in which he did not join, and a cold chill of apprehension sent a tingle along Rane's spine as she looked up at last and met his icy stare, that warned her she would account to him for her temerity before the evening drew to a close.

It dragged on, through an endless supper, some of which Rane forced herself to swallow to counteract the effects of the champagne. The ploy was successful, and the effervescence vanished like a burst champagne bubble; black depression took its place, sitting upon her spiirits like a cloud and making her long for an excuse to escape the rest of the party.

'Are you enjoying the dance, Marie?' She found herself next to the elderly dresser, and forced herself to speak with false brightness.

'I do not dance,' the Frenchwoman responded frigidly, and Rane sighed. Obviously she was not yet forgiven for the ruined suit, and for suggesting that Leo should design the wedding dress, but now was not the time to make amends. She moved away despondently, wishing she was on the other side of the room nearer to the door so that she could slip away unnoticed. Her depression deepened at the conviction that she would, indeed, go unnoticed. Leo danced cheek to cheek with Marion, both of them oblivious to all except the other. Zilla danced with Jack the groom who, in the absence of a more suitable male, was handsome enough to engage her attention, if not wealthy enough to command her permanent interest. Greville danced with Shelley.

They made a handsome couple, the girl nearly as tall as the man. Greville's dark head bent low over his partner, making a perfect foil for the mannequin's ash-blonde hair, and his face was intent, listening to something she was saying. Shelley was an amusing conversationalist, and they both burst out laughing, happy, shared laughter, at some secret joke between the two of them, while Greville swung her gaily round in the gyrations of the dance. The two were perfecty matched. Rane watched them miserably, the tall, slender girl with her enviable mannequin's figure; the taller, handsome man, with his slim-hipped athlete's frame. Tears stung Rane's eyes as she watched them execute a tango together with an accomplished skill that would do justice to an exhibition dance. They glided to a halt as the music

stopped, and a ripple of applause ran across the
room. Rane turned away and buried her face in her
glass of champagne to hide the two slow tears that
escaped her lashes and trickled down her cheeks to
join the wine in her glass.

'If you gulp champagne like that, it'll go straight to
your legs.'

Greville's hand reached round her and removed the
glass from her fingers, to put it down on a nearby
table, then transferred his hand to her waist and drew
her with him on to the floor, and unbelievably they
were dancing together again, and it seemed as if they
had never stopped, that his dance with Shelley was
simply a part of a dream, and this was the only,
wonderful reality. From somewhere, a chiming clock
said it must be the last dance of the evening, the
proverbial last waltz.

'I know, now, how Cinderella must have felt,' said
Rane. But the chimes of midnight passed, and her
dress remained unchanged, and Greville's coach was a
real one, not a pumpkin.

'You're talking nonsense. You need a breath of fresh
air, the champagne's gone to your head.'

He said it would go to her legs. She giggled weakly
because it had gone in the opposite direction, then
suddenly it did not seem funny any more, and she
wanted to cry. She made no attempt to resist as he
danced her towards the door and out of the room into
the dimly lit hall. She caught a glimpse of the suit of
armour, gleaming metallically in the subdued light,
then he swung her to a halt at the foot of the stairs,
with her back to the sturdy newel-post. He reached
round her and gripped the wood with both his hands,
so that his arms were on each side of her effectively
preventing her from moving away as he demanded
abruptly,

'Why did you couple Leo and Marion together in your toast tonight?'

The newel-post was hard against her back. His arms were ramrod-hard on either side of her, and his voice was harder still as he repeated harshly,

'Why?'

The edge of the post cut into her shoulders, sharp as the edge of anger in his vice, and Rane raised her hands to her throat as an instinctive, defensive gesture against the anger, while her eyes stared upwards into his, wide pools of apprehension in her upturned face.

'Tell me?' He stared implacably down at her, impatient at her silence. His hands left the post and gripped her wrists, then he pulled her towards him and gave her a shake, as if he would shake the words from out of her speechless mouth.

'Tell me!'

'Loose my wrists, you're hurting me!' she gasped. The sudden jerk of his shake, the pain from his fierce grip, shocked her into speech as he had meant it should. It shocked her into something more, into angry retaliation that swept aside the fear that gripped her, unlocking her tongue so that words spilled from her in a furious spate, tipped with venom, and aimed to wound.

'Why shouldn't I couple Marion and Leo together?' she cried shrilly. 'They're in love.' Furiously she justified her action.

'They're not engaged.'

'They will be.'

'Not unless I give my consent,' Greville grated. 'By your action tonight, you practically advertised their engagement as a fait accompli.'

'It will be soon, with or without your consent,' Rane taunted him recklessly.

'Marion will rue the day she defies me,' he growled threateningly.

'How like a man!' Rane glared up at him, incensed by his unyielding attitude. 'You'll ruin her engagement, spoil what should be the happiest day of her life, simply because she won't conform to the pattern you set for her!'

'Marion's my ward, I'm responsible for her.'

'She's your ward, not your property!' Rane hammered at him, and felt as bruised as if she was hammering at the flint walls of Fullcote Hall itself. 'You can't own people, the same as you own diamonds,' she told him forcefully.

'Diamonds are a lot less trouble to look after than human beings,' he retorted grimly, and without warning he released her wrists. Deprived of his support, Rane swayed backwards, caught off balance, and she grasped behind her at the newel-post to save herself from falling.

'I warned you the champagne would go to your legs,' Greville misunderstood her unsteadiness, and put out a quick hand to grasp her shoulder.

'Half a glass of champagne isn't enough to upset anyone's balance.' His hand on her shoulder was doing far worse things to her equlibrium than any amount of champagne was capable of. She felt weak, with a craven weakness that made her fingers long to lock themselves round his hand, draw it down from her shoulders, and caress it in both of her own. Her hands even made a small upwards movement in the direction of her shoulder, and she checked them sharply, appalled at her own lack of self-control, forcing her fingers instead to wrap themselves round her own ill-used wrists, and gripping them with a force that was more painful by far than that which Greville had used.

'Do they hurt?' His quick eyes caught her movement, interpreted it, and again drew the wrong conclusions. 'You should have spoken when I asked you. . . .'

'Is that what Marion can expect if she defies you?' Rane's overwrought nerves gave way, and she shouted up at him hysterically, 'Can she expect bruises, too, if she doesn't do as she's told?' Her heart held more bruises than her wrists, and from the depths of its pain she struck out blindly, seeking to assuage the agony by inflicting hurt in return.

'Marion can't be expected to know her own mind, she's only nineteen.'

'She knows her own mind about one thing, and that's the birthday photograph I promised her,' Rane revealed rashly. 'She wants one of herself and Leo together, and I intend to take it for her,' she finished defiantly.

The foil was off and the rapier point was needle-sharp, and she lunged without mercy, only the throbbing pulse at the point of Greville's tightly clenched jaw telling her the thrust had gone home.

'If it's a good photograph, I'll take a copy for myself,' he snarled.

'I'll send you the proof.' She twisted the blade, pulled it free and thrust again. 'Then you and I will each have a souvenir to keep!'

Swiftly she ducked under his arm, breaking free from his grip, and ran for the stairs. He made no attempt to pursue her, but stood like a statue beside the newel-post, his eyes marking her flight. Rane felt them bore into her back as she fled, but she refused to turn round, and with shaking hands she grasped at the banister rail and pulled herself along, forcing her palsied legs to carry her upwards, while she realised, with a fury that mounted with each stumbling step, that she had just told Greville something else he wanted to know. That she had not only found the photograph he rescued from the lake and left in her room, but that she intended to keep it as a souvenir.

CHAPTER NINE

'WILL it look better with the hat, or without it, do you think?' Shelley viewed her reflection critically in the ornate mirror.

Another day. Another photography session. Another opportunity to immerse herself in work, and to forget, if such a thing was possible, the sleepless hours of mental anguish that left Rane as reluctant to face the dawn as she was to meet Greville again.

'Hold it like that, just as you are.' Professional discipline presented her with a saving armour, and Rane donned it gratefully, although her heart winced away from the elegant reflection presented by Shelley in the mirror.

'If only I were tall!' she sighed to herself wistfully. She felt small and insignificant, surrounded by such queenly height. If she was tall, there would be more of her for Greville to notice. She would more nearly match his own height. She thrust down the traitorous thoughts and ducked her head over her camera to disguise the sudden moistness that forced her to blink rapidly before Shelley came back into focus in the view-finder.

'Keep your arms raised as if you're putting the hat on,' she urged the mannequin. 'It shows the fit of the suit jacket to perfection when you do that.'

'There's no need to use clips on it this time,' Shelley quipped wickedly, and Rane groaned aloud.

'Don't remind me!' she begged. The re-made sage green silk suit hugged Shelley's figure as if she had been poured into it, her upraised arms adjusting the hat at an angle on her smoothly coiffured head, emphasised the figure-hugging lines of the jacket, sleekly plain at the front and dropping into a neatly pleated peplum at the back, softly rounded to give the figure added curve.

'It was a good idea of yours to photograph this suit in the mirror,' Shelley remarked appreciatively. 'The picture will show the detail of the back, and the front view, at the same time.'

'I want the best of both worlds,' Rane returned swiftly, and felt her heart contract. She wanted Greville, and the agonising hours of the previous night had brought her no closer to coming to terms with the knowledge than it had brought her sleep.

'Will that do, Rane? My arms are ready to drop off!' Shelley wailed.

'Sorry.' Rane flushed guiltily. 'I thought the shutter had seized, but it seems to have freed itself again,' she lied hastily. 'It was a bit of grit, I expect.' In truth she had forgotten Shelley standing with her arms upraised, putting on the hat. Her mind had seized on the one inescapable fact that sooner or later she would have to come to terms with, whatever the consequences to herself, and her eyes and her throat felt gritty at the prospect of the hopeless struggle ahead.

'I'd better take some more shots, just in case.' She took several for the sake of appearances, with the hat on, with the hat off, with the jacket draped across a chair, and knew she would not use any of them, because the first photograph taken in front of the mirror eclipsed them all.

'What a good idea.' Marion appeared and remained to watch, intrigued by the skilful use of the mirror to portray the detail on both sides of the suit at the same time.

'It's an old trick of the trade,' Rane smiled, 'but it

makes a pleasing picture that's just that little bit different. I could do one of you in the same way if you like,' she suggested accommodatingly. 'If you sit on a chair somewhere about here,' she placed herself, and squinted in the mirror consideringly. 'The carved table and the grandfather clock by the door would make an interesting background reflection. I'll take several shots of you in different poses, and you can choose the one you like best for your birthday present.'

'I already know which one I shall like best,' Marion blushed prettily. 'It'll be the one of Leo and me together.'

Rane already knew that, too, so why had she suggested taking half a dozen more, of Marion on her own? Not for Leo, he would share Marion's picture of the two of them together. Not for Greville, she defended her action fiercely to herself. He had said he would have a copy if there was one good enough, but she had definitely not suggested taking more because of Greville. And yet for who else?

'I'll go and fetch Leo, he and Marie were fussing about with hemlines when I came downstairs, and if I don't drag him away he'll be there all day,' Marion exclaimed. 'I'll leave my ring on the table here, and put it on when I come back. I'd like it to show in the photograph.'

'Young love . . .!' Shelley raised expressive eyes ceilingwards, and gave a wry grimace as she added, 'I'll have to go upstairs as well and hand this suit back to Marie, and reassure her it's still intact.'

'That'll release Leo for a while at least,' Rane observed with satisfaction, and the mannequin laughed.

'Marie wants me for the rest of the morning, to start modelling the toile of the wedding dress. Oh yes, she's

got it well started,' she answered Rane's look of
surprise at her announcement.

'She must have stayed up most of the night,' Rane
exclaimed in awe.

'From the state of her temper I imagine she
remained up *all* night,' Shelley gloomed, 'and because
she hasn't got the usual wooden dummy to fit the toile
on to, she's making do with me. Who'd double for a
wooden dummy?' she grumbled her way out of the
room, but Rane was too busy to heed her complaints.
She tried the chair in various positions in front of the
mirror, with a keen eye to placing it on exactly the
right spot to make the best use of the available
background.

'This is about right,' she decided aloud at last. The
old clock, and the even older table, both standing just
inside the open door of heavy oak, would make the
perfect contrast to the fresh, modern loveliness of
nineteen years old. She put her eye to the view-finder.

'Oh, bother!' Without thinking she pressed the
shutter button, bewailing her own carelessness in
wasting film. 'I shall probably have a photograph of
half of you,' she joked as her eye caught a slight
movement in the region of the door. 'Come and try
this position, and see if you like the reflected
background, Marion.' She turned towards the door
and raised her head from her camera.

'Marion?' A puzzled frown creased her forehead. 'I
could have sworn. . . .' she muttered. 'Oh, there you
are,' as Marion appeared in the doorway dragging Leo
by the hand.

'Sorry we've been such an age,' she apologised
cheerfully. 'Leo was immersed in hemlines, as usual.'

'Never mind, now you're here, come and sit
together, and let's begin.' Rane seated the couple, and
took a shot of them together on a nearby settee; a more

natural one with Leo relaxed in an armchair and
Marion sitting on the rug at his feet, gazing up
adoringly into his face. She did not need to pose for
that one, Rane thought with a smile, and took several
more in different positions that would give the girl a
wide selection from which to choose her birthday gift.
Marion's training as a mannequin made the work easy.
Leo presented more difficulty, being more camera-
shy, but willing to do anything to make Marion happy,
and the photography session proceeded pleasantly so
that Rane was almost sorry when it came to an end.

'Now come and sit in this chair in front of the
mirror, for one last shot,' she urged Marion.

'On my own?' Her subject was patently reluctant to
leave Leo out of any of the shots.

'Leo might like one special shot of just you on your
own,' Rane suggested slyly. If Greville wanted a copy
of Marion's birthday photograph, he was unlikely to
want one portraying Leo as well, though she tried to
convince herself that it was for the latter's benefit, and
not for Greville, that she wanted to take the extra shot.

'Of course, I never thought of that.' The smile
returned to Marion's face. 'Let me put on my ring
first.' She turned happily enough to retrieve it from
the table.

'Put it on and come and pose for me.' Rane pointed
her camera mirror-wards and busied herself in
working out angles. There was a long pause, then
Marion spoke again, and asked in a peculiar voice,

'Did you move my ring, Rane, while I was out of
the room?'

'Move it? No, why should I move it? Didn't you put
it on the table when you went upstairs to collect Leo?'
Rane asked vaguely, her mind more on the immediate
demands of her work than on what Marion was saying.

'I put the ring box on the table by the door, but it

isn't there any more.' The nineteen-year-old's voice was strained. 'My ring's gone,' she said flatly.

The silence seemed to last for a long time, then Leo and Rane both spoke together.

'It can't have gone!'

'Perhaps you slipped it on your finger without thinking.' Rane put down her camera and reached for the girl's hands. Her fingers were unadorned.

'How could I have been so careless?' Marion's eyes were over-bright, and there was a distinct catch in her voice.

'Nonsense,' Rane replied robustly. 'You don't expect to have to guard your possessions in your own home. Perhaps one of the maids saw it lying on the table, and thought you'd mislaid it. Why, she might even be looking for you now, to give it back to you,' she comforted.

'Was Ellen in here, doing the dusting?' Brief hope lit Marion's face.

'No, I didn't see her. I didn't see anybody after you and Shelley left, until you came back with Leo,' Rane confessed, and wished from the crestfallen look on Marion's face she had not tried to comfort her in the first place.

'If your ring's really missing, the best thing to do is to let Greville know, and start searching for it right away,' Leo suggested reluctantly. 'The sooner it's found the better.' Patently he was more concerned with Marion's distress than with the missing valuable.

'I daren't tell Greville, he'll be furious if he knows I've lost it,' Marion protested.

'What is it you've lost, and why should I be furious?' Greville strolled into the room to join them, and to Rane's consternation, Zilla was with him.

'I've been looking for you, to give you these. They came in the post this morning.' Greville handed his ward a couple of envelopes that looked as if they might contain belated birthday cards. 'Now tell me what's the matter,' he urged, and thus pressured, Marion blurted out unhappily,

'It's my ring. I put it down for a few minutes while I went upstairs to fetch Leo, and now it's gone!' She gulped to a halt.

'What, not that lovely ruby ring you had for your birthday?' Zilla exclaimed in shocked tones.

'It wasn't a ruby, it was a sapphire, surrounded by diamonds,' Greville corrected her, and Rane's lips thinned.

Zilla knew full well it was a sapphire. Rane had seen Marion showing the ring to her the previous evening, and the older mannequin making a close examination of the jewel. Costing it, Rane thought cynically at the time, and doubtless discovering that the total value of the rings on her own much bejewelled fingers did not amount to one tithe of the value of the single jewel adorning Marion's. With Zilla's love of jewellery it was impossible to believe she would mistake a sapphire for a ruby.

'She's just saying it to gain Greville's attention.' And succeeding, with her usual adroitness, Rane realised with rising impatience. Trust Zilla to make the most of the situation, regardless of Marion's distress.

'Where did you actually leave the ring?' Greville's tone justified Marion's reluctance to say anything to him, and Rane felt herself shiver on the girl's behalf.

'On the table, here, by the door. Oh, Greville, what shall I do?' Marion wailed.

'Answer my questions to start with,' he retorted, and plied her with another one.

'Was the door open?'

'Yes, just as it is now.'

'And who was in the room with you at the time?'

'Rane and Shelley, and then Shelley and I went upstairs together. . . .'

'And left Rane on her own in the room,' Zilla murmured, and her look and her voice were loaded with venom. 'How strange, that Rane should be there when Leo's designs went missing, and now she's on the scene again just when your ring disappears,' she purred maliciously.

'That's an infamous thing to say! How dare you insinuate. . . .' Rane exploded wrathfully.

'Nobody's insinuating anything,' Greville cut her short abruptly. 'We'll institute a thorough search for the ring, and if it's merely been mislaid it should soon turn up. If it doesn't. . . .' he stopped significantly.

'If it doesn't, presumably you'll telephone for the police,' Zilla finished for him, with a barbed look in Rane's direction.

'I doubt if that'll be necessary,' Greville retorted discouragingly, and Zilla lapsed into silence, but Rane's mind was in a whirl.

Whatever Greville said, the insinuation was there, spoken out loud, and if the thought had not been in the minds of Marion and Leo, or even Greville himself beforehand, Zilla had put it there now, a seed sown, and probably, Rane thought blackly, already beginning to germinate. At that moment she felt she hated Zilla. Almost as much as she hated Greville. She faced them defensively, a tiny figure dwarfed by the tallness of the other four, who were all regarding her, she felt bleakly certain, with mounting suspicion. It was there in their faces, their eyes.

'If you think I've taken the ring, why don't you start your search by searching me?' Baldly she put into words what she felt convinced must be in the minds of the other three, as well as Zilla.

'Don't be silly!' Greville's tone was peremptory.

'It's not being silly to resent the suggestion that I took the ring!' Rane blazed.

'Nobody's suggesting anything of the kind, and nobody in my house will.' Greville's look sent a straight warning to Zilla, but Rane was too incensed to notice a message that was not aimed directly at herself.

'Nobody in your house—but the police might. Is that what you mean?' She put her own construction on his choice of words, and turned on him like a tiny tigress, defending her good name.

'All this argument isn't getting us anywhere.' Marion began to sob. 'It isn't helping to bring back my ring.'

'I'll look for your ring, *ma chérie*. Don't worry, it'll turn up.' Despite Greville's presence, Leo put his arm comfortingly about her shoulders.

'Take her upstairs to Shelley and Marie, Leo. We'll have a search in the area of the table here, in case the ring's simply dropped on to the floor and slid under something.' Greville formed an unexpected alliance with the Frenchman, to take Marion out of the way.

'I hadn't thought of that. Maybe it's rolled against the wainscoting, or under the clock.' Quick hope dropped Rane to her knees on the floor, and she ducked under the table and ignored Zilla's sneer.

'Scrabble about on the floor if you want to, it can't hurt your old jersey and slacks. I refuse to risk laddering my stockings,' she pouted.

'It isn't anywhere near the wainscoting.'

'I'll have a look under the clock.'

Two things happened with disconcerting suddenness. Greville dropped on his hands and knees and joined Rane under the table, and Zilla sat on top of it and dangled her sheer-clad legs over the edge.

For Greville's benefit, Rane deduced sourly, and

suppressed a giggle when Greville turned his back on the mannequin's beautifully shaped extremities and bent all his attention to searching under the clock, and against the wainscoting.

'I've already looked there,' Rane snapped, her momentary humour deserting her. Did he think she was looking, or merely pretending to look?

'In that case, we'll look on the other side of the table. If we can manage to get out from under it,' he added drily, and swung round on his knees to face her. 'You'll have to back out,' he told Rane gravely, 'and I'll follow.' Zilla's dangling legs barred the way he had come in, and short of upsetting her from on top of the table—Rane felt a dreadful temptation to do just that—there was only one exit for them both. 'Back away,' Greville urged her, 'I'll steer you.'

He shuffled forward on his knees, and his face came close to her own, and if she had not known better she could have mistaken the glint in his eyes for one of pure schoolboy mischief. He gave only the briefest of glances at the provocatively dangling legs, then he turned back to face Rane, and the schoolboy vanished, and his face, so close to her own that she could feel the faint, soft wind of his breath upon her forehead; his face was all man, and his eyes held her, with a look in them that she could not read, and suddenly did not dare to try. For a timeless second she stared back at him, her own eyes wide, and then he moved, and the move brought his face even closer until it hovered just a fraction of an inch above her own, close enough to. . . .

Rane's courage broke, and she scuttled backwards like a frightened rabbit and pushed herself shakily to her feet.

'Ouch!'

Her haste was her undoing. Her shuffle had not

quite cleared the edge of the table, and it gave her a sharp crack on the head as she rose. Dizzily she put a hand on to the table top to steady herself. She felt rather than saw Greville emerge from under the table and rise to his feet beside her, and then his hand gripped her shoulder and his voice asked concernedly.

'Are you all right, Rane?'

'Yes. Yes, I'm fine.' She did not lie. The effect of his touch was electric. It shocked her out of her daze and into instant awareness of Greville, of Zilla, of her own hand resting on the table top.

'The hand. . . .' Her dizziness forgotten, she spun to face Greville. 'I remember now!' she cried excitedly. 'I saw a hand reach through the doorway!'

'Yes, all right. You saw a hand.' His voice was soothing, and Rane's patience snapped.

'I'm not concussed, if that's what you're thinking,' she denied angrily. 'I tell you, I *did* see a hand. It was after Marion and Shelley left the room. I was trying out angles in the mirror for a reflected photograph, and I saw a hand reach in at the doorway, and across to the table. That must have been when the ring was taken. It was only the merest glimpse. I thought it was Marion at the time, I spoke to her and wondered why she didn't answer.'

'Now she tells us.' Zilla coolly lit a cigarette and blew the smoke in Rane's direction, and added with patent disbelief. 'A hand, indeed! That's a likely story, I must say.'

'It's true, I tell you! I haven't made it up. I can pr. . . .' Rane stopped. With perfect clarity she remembered seeing the movement of the hand. With equal clarity she remembered accidentally pressing the shutter button of her camera. In spite of her excuse to Shelley about grit jamming the shutter, she knew her equipment was in perfect working order, and in one illuminating flash it dawned upon her that her carelessness in handling the camera might give her just the evidence she needed to prove her own innocence.

'I can pr. . . .' Some instinct of caution stopped her from declaring her proof. Film could be faulty, and a camera could misfire, and if it did, her proof would look like just another excuse, and probably have the opposite effect and incriminate her for ever in Greville's eyes.

'Take these films for me to Clive Redman on your way back to town, Shelley.' The travesty of lunch was over, and the afternoon was well advanced when the mannequin appeared downstairs, coated and scarfed in readiness for her journey back to London. 'Tell Clive to pull out all the stops to give you the proofs to bring back with you tomorrow morning,' she begged. 'If Marion has her photographs to choose from, it'll take her mind off the loss of her ring.' Not even to Shelley would Rane reveal her true reason for wanting the proofs back so urgently.

'I shan't return here until about this time tomorrow,' Shelley answered, 'so it'll give Clive plenty of time to get the film processed and the results ready for me to collect when I start out just before lunch.'

'I thought you'd be here immediately after breakfast, the same as usual.' Rane stared at her companion, nonplussed. How was she to bear the delay, the suspicion, until later afternoon tomorrow? 'I can't ask Zilla to take them, even if she was going back to town today.' Unconsciously she spoke her thoughts out loud.

'Zilla's already gone back to town.' Shelley eyed Rane curiously. 'I thought you knew? I saw her come out of Greville's study immediately after lunch, and her face was like thunder. They must have had a row of some sort, because Zilla ran upstairs and came back with her things, and then she went off in her car, driving like the wind. I thought you'd know what it was all about?' she quizzed Rane hopefully.

'Zilla? A row with Greville?' Rane echoed, perplexed. 'They seemed good enough friends before lunch. Perhaps Greville took her to task because she wouldn't help to look for Marion's ring, and she took offence and went off in a huff,' she hazarded, and added resignedly, 'I expect she'll change her mind before she's got very far, and come back again.' When Zilla was playing for high stakes, she would not allow a row with the biggest stake of all—Greville—to stand in her way.

'From the expression on Greville's face when he followed her out of his study, I doubt if she'll get the chance to change her mind,' Shelley chuckled. 'She's shot her bolt in that direction, I reckon,' she guessed graphically. 'But at least it's left her bedroom free for the two seamstresses to use.'

'What seamstresses?' Events were happening at a speed that left Rane struggling to keep up.

'Two girls are being flown in from the workrooms in Paris, to make up the wedding gown, no less,' Shelley imparted her news with relish.

'So soon?' Rane gasped incredulously.

'So soon,' Shelley confirmed, well satisfied with the effect of her news. 'Marie's worked miracles on the toile, and when the girls arrive I imagine they'll be expected to do the same with the actual dress. They're due to arrive at any minute now,' she glanced at the tiny watch on her wrist, 'and they'll be bringing with them the material Leo ordered by telephone from Paris. That sounds as if it might be their taxi outside now.' She cocked her head to one side as the unmistakable rattle of a diesel engine shattered the afternoon silence. 'Here comes Leo, he must have heard it, too,' as the Frenchman came running downstairs and made for the front door. 'I'm going,' Shelley decided, 'before they find me another job to do. See you tomorrow, Rane. I won't forget your photographs.'

Shelley vanished, and Leo reappeared through the door talking volubly to two neatly clad girls whom he ushered straight upstairs, from where Rane heard him calling for Marie.

'My home is beginning to resemble a walk-around store,' Greville grumbled in her right ear, and Rane started and spun round, and scowled at the beginnings of a grin that tilted the corners of his well-cut lips, mocking her sudden fright.

'If I jump out of my skin every time Greville speaks to me, he'll think I've got a guilty conscience,' Rane berated herself fiercely, and retorted in a voice sharpened by fright,

'Shelley and Zilla have already gone, and you'll be rid of the rest of us by the weekend, then you can have the house to yourself again.'

'And welcome,' she added sourly to herself, and wished she had the courage to say it out loud, but something in Greville's expression stopped her, something that had been in his eyes under the table, and lurked in them again now. Something she could not name, but which sent a tingling excitement coursing through her and rooted her feet to the floor as he stepped directly in front of her and asked smoothly,

'Are you intending to follow Zilla and Shelley?'

'I might be, and I might not,' she retorted defensively. If she was, she would be obliged to walk right round him, since he was positioned between her and the door. Deliberately barring her exit?

'Making sure I can't escape,' Rane realised angrily.

'He still suspects I might have the ring on me.' Aloud she declared, 'I'll go and find my car keys, and decide what I'm going to do then.' She faced him defiantly, asserting her right to leave if she chose, putting to the test her fear that he might try to prevent her from doing so.

'Your keys are probably in your slacks pocket.' Before she could step away from him, Greville put out both his hands and clapped them against her slacks pockets, feeling for the bulge of her keys. Or feeling for the ring box?

'How dare you try to search me!'

She forgot that she had earlier invited him to do just that. She forgot everything except her outrage and shame, and the searing humiliation of being searched in the house to which she came as an invited guest.

'How dare you!' she choked. A tide of furious indignation brought scarlet colour rushing to her cheeks and brought her hand up impulsively to slap his. Without pausing to think she struck blindly upwards, but before the blow could land his fingers trapped her wrist in a steel grip.

'You're talking nonsense again,' he accused her harshly. 'I was searching for your car keys.'

'Don't lie to me!' she spat at him, and her eyes flashed fire up at his set face. 'You think I took the ring. You think because I had the opportunity, I couldn't resist the temptation!' With frenzied strength she broke his grip and turned blindly to run, unable to see in which direction for the scalding tears that poured down her now ashen cheeks.

'Look where you're going!'

She looked, but she could not see. Her toes stubbed hard against the bottom of a wooden plinth, her flailing arms wrapped themselves round armour plating in a desperate attempt to keep her balance, and with a metallic crash that echoed through the house, the suit of armour collapsed on top of her and strewed its component parts across the hall floor. Its component parts, and something else. Hardly aware of what she was doing, Rane reached down and gathered together the papers that the rolling helmet spewed over the floor.

'Leo's sketches!' she whispered wonderingly. 'The missing Harvest Designs. I thought Gus Crawford. . . .' No wonder the designs had not appeared in the *Echo* if they had been hidden in the suit of armour all the time!

'As I thought, your journalist had bigger fish in mind,' Greville's tone was almost absent. 'He got wind of the diamond and came sniffing round to try and discover if the rumours he heard were true. He wasn't interested in Leo's sketches.' He reached out and took them from her hand. 'So that's where they were. Why didn't I think of it before?' he exclaimed. 'It's the perfect hiding place, and so simple. So quick. Just pop them through the vizor like posting letters in a pillar box.' Abruptly he stopped talking and did something quite inexplicable, and Rane stared at him in amazement as he picked up one armour-plated boot and turned it upside down and shook it, then when that did not produce the results he appeared to be looking for, he repeated the performance with its fellow. A faint knocking sound rewarded the shake this time, and when he upended the boot something small and hard fell out of it. A box. A leather-covered jeweller's box.

'Marion's ring!' Rane gasped.

Greville flicked open the box, and the sapphire and its satellite diamonds winked back at them solemnly.

'It was the perfect hiding place!' Greville exclaimed again, and his eyes met Rane's in a blaze of triumph.

'You needn't congratulate me,' she cried, needled by the implication. 'I didn't use it. And now you've found the sketches and the ring,' she followed up vigorously, 'you can start looking for the person who stole them. You know now that it wasn't Gus Crawford, and it certainly wasn't me. And if you're still in any doubt,' she swept on as Greville made as if to speak, 'take a good look at the suit of armour when it's restored to its plinth, and ask yourself how I could have posted anything through the vizor in that helmet,' she gave the headgear a contemptuous kick with her toe as it lay on the floor at her feet. 'It was way above my head when it stood upright, I should have needed a stepladder to reach it,' she exaggerated wildly, and spinning on her heel she fled for her room, grateful for the first time in her life for her erstwhile lamented lack of inches.

CHAPTER TEN

'HERE are your proofs, Rane. And Clive Redman said to tell you that even for you, they're quite good. Catch!' Shelley tossed the editor's sally and his package towards her, and ran upstairs in answer to Marie's impatient call.

'Thanks.' In her anxiety Rane nearly dropped the package. She grabbed, missed, and grabbed again, successfully this time, and tore open the wrapping with trembling fingers, unable to wait even to sit down before looking at the contents.

The first set of proofs were of Shelley, modelling the Summer Collection. They were superlatively good, especially the one taken in the mirror, but Rane spared them hardly a glance. Tensely she riffled through them, one after the other. Where was the one she had taken of the hand? The photograph she had taken accidentally?

The proofs of Shelley's modelling session came to an end, and Marion's face looked up at Rane from the next set, from the settee with Leo, from the floor looking up at Leo.

'Where . . .?' Rane quivered with impatience. A knot tightened at the back of her neck, tensing her shoulder muscles, and with a steady, insistent drumbeat her head began to throb.

'Where . . .?'

Frantically she turned over proof after proof.

'Of course,' she exclaimed at last, 'it was the middle picture, after Shelley, and before I started to take shots of Marion and Leo.' It had to be the middle picture because that was the order in which it was taken, and the print room superintendent had packed the proofs in reverse order in the packs. Rane fanned through them eagerly, and with trembling fingers picked out the one she was looking for.

'The hand!' she breathed with satisfaction. 'I knew I'd seen it. I knew I wasn't mistaken!' She dropped into a chair and allowed the other photographs to fall unheeded on to the table in front of her, and stared at the one she had taken accidentally. It was all the proof she needed. The hand was there, reaching out towards the table top, towards the ring box that showed up clearly on the print. A hand, and part of an arm. But whose? Rane wrinkled her brows perplexedly.

'These are good.' Greville strolled into the room and reached out for the photographs lying on the table, but this time his soft-footed approach did not make Rane start, she was too intent on studying the picture of the hand. Out of the corner of her eye she saw and noted Greville's hand reach towards the photographs on the table, and unconsciously she shook her head. The hand in her picture did not belong to Greville. It belonged to a woman. The fingers were long and slim, and beautifully manicured, and one of them bore a large, ornate ring. Rane stared at the ring, and something clicked in her memory. She had watched that same ring before, across the dinner table, was it a lifetime ago? her eyes attracted by the flash of brilliants to the hand that wore it. To the dark smudge that stained the gripping side of the wearer's index finger. She caught a painful breath.

'Zilla!' she exclaimed softly. Was there no limit to the mannequin's spite? And all because she, Rane, had taken a carriage ride with Greville.

'I'd like a copy of one of these, when Marion's taken her choice.' Numbly Rane registered the surprising

fact that Greville did not ask for a photograph of
Shelley, not even of the one taken in the mirror, that
showed her lovely, laughing face to perfection, as well
as the suit she was wearing.

'You can have the lot for all I care, but take a look at
this one first.' With quick fingers Rane skimmed the
proof across the table towards Greville. The paper
made a faint hissing sound as it skated across the
polished wood, loud in the suddenly pregnant silence.

'I told you I saw a hand reach through the door
towards Marion's ring box on the table.' With an
immense effort she managed to keep her voice low, but
her fingers gripped the edge of the table in front of
her, and she rose to her feet, and her knuckles showed
white against the dark oak. 'I told you I thought it was
Marion coming into the room, and when I turned to
speak to her I accidentally pressed the shutter button
on my camera. That's the picture it took,' she gestured
towards the proof which came to rest within an inch of
Greville's grasp. 'It's a picture of someone else's hand,
not mine,' she emphasised clearly. 'I couldn't possibly
be behind the camera and picking up the ring box at
the same time, could I?' she questioned him tautly.
She refused to tell him whose hand it was. 'Let him
discover the culprit for himself,' she decided hardly.
She had proved her own innocence, and that was
enough. In a few days she would be back in London,
and the ring, and Greville, and the whole unhappy
episode would be nothing but a bad memory.

'I didn't say you took the ring.' Greville spoke, and
his voice was as quiet as her own.

'Now you *know* I didn't,' Rane retorted unforgiv-
ingly. 'Now you can find out who did!' Tension
rasped at the edges of her self-control, and her voice
began to waver.

'I already know who did. This,' Greville flicked the

picture with one finger, 'this merely confirms that my suspicions were correct.'

Oh, the self-assurance of the man, to so calmly accept that he was always correct!

'Which is why I sent Zilla packing immediately after lunch,' he continued evenly. 'Whatever I felt about her outrageous behaviour, I could hardly refuse her lunch.' His lips tilted with the beginnings of a grin. 'Even a condemned prisoner is given a meal,' he pointed out reasonably.

'You really *did* know!' Rane stared up at him, her eyes enormous in her white face, incredulity struggling with anger at this proof that he had, indeed, known beforehand. 'You knew, and you still allowed me to think. . . .' The anger won, and she choked to a halt, while the green anguish of her eyes condemned him for knowing, and for still allowing her to suffer.

'I thought you must know as well.' It was Greville's turn to show surprise. 'You told me you'd seen a hand, and with the quantity of rings Zilla habitually wears on her fingers, I thought you couldn't possibly mistake who it belonged to.'

'I only caught a glimpse. I couldn't be sure.'

Suddenly she could not be sure of the look in Greville's eyes, either. They held her own with an expression lurking in them that she had seen before, not once but several times.

'I never for a moment suspected you. You must believe that, Rane.'

Suddenly, joyfully, she did believe him. She opened her mouth to tell him so, then closed it again, the words unuttered, as he stopped speaking and began to move slowly round the edge of the table towards her, his hand gathering up the photographs as he came, while his eyes held her fixedly, never once leaving her face.

'You must believe me.'

Rane watched him, fascinated. It seemed as if she was turned to stone, only her wildly throbbing pulse was alive, hammering a tattoo in time with his steady footfalls round the table. Her hand still gripped its edge, holding on to it now for support to prop up knees that unaccountably began to shake.

'Shall we destroy this proof?' He held up the incriminating photograph between finger and thumb, as if even to touch it was offensive to him. 'We don't need to take the matter any further, now the ring and the sketches have been recovered. Zilla didn't take them in order to keep them for herself, she only removed them to spite you, hoping you'd be blamed.'

'How did you guess?' Rane's head was in a whirl.

'It wasn't difficult,' Greville answered her gravely. 'I heard her bedroom door close when we returned to the house on the night you went journalist-hunting with Leo.' He smiled at the memory, quietly amused by the episode. 'You must have heard it too.'

She had heard the door close upstairs, but she had not put the same construction on the sound as Greville evidently had. In fact, she had forgotten all about it until now.

'When Leo's sketches went missing, I put two and two together after I realised that Zilla was madly jealous of you.'

'Jealous of me?' Rane echoed incredulously. 'Why should she be jealous of me?' Zilla had everything she had not—exotic looks, fabulous clothes to model, queenly height. Plus Greville's attention, she remembered unhappily. 'Why?'

'Can't you guess?' Greville asked her softly, and came to a halt in front of her, closing in on her so that her back was against the table and his arms pinned her to it on either side, and the faint smell of his after-

shave lotion wafted round her as he leaned over her
and invited teasingly,

'Have a guess.'

She could not guess, not in a thousand years. She
dared not guess. Her breath came in tiny, panting
gasps through her softly parted lips, an open invitation
to his as they hovered over her.

'Have a guess.'

'Rane, where are you? Has Jack brought the carriage
round yet? We're ready to start!'

Shelley's voice. Shelley herself, dressed in the bridal
gown, ready to model it for Rane's camera. Why, oh,
why did she have to choose this particular moment?

'Have a guess. . . .'

She dared not guess, in case her answer might prove
to be wrong. And if she failed to guess, would Greville
have supplied her with the answer? She would never
know, now. She stared dully at Shelley as the
mannequin ran lightly into the room, enveloped in a
cloud of white.

'We've locked Marion in her bedroom, so she can't
see the dress,' she laughed. 'If she saw it, she'd want
to try it on, and it's unlucky for Leo to see her in it
before the wedding day.'

More unlucky still for Rane to see Shelley in it, at
the one moment in time when she most needed to be
alone with Greville. It seemed a symbol of her evil
luck that Shelley should model a wedding gown such
as she herself would never wear. It was Greville, or
nobody, for her. Slowly Rane stood up, releasing her
hold on the table, prising herself loose finger by
painful finger, each one stiff with the strain of
gripping, and fearful to loose in case her trembling
legs should fail to hold her upright.

'I've got the carriage outside, miss. We're ready
when you are.' Jack eyed Shelley admiringly.

'Coming right away,' she smiled back at him. 'Ready, Rane?'

'Yes, I'm ready,' she answered automatically. She was as ready as she would ever be to photograph a wedding dress intended for another bride.

'Take the first shot of Shelley stepping out of the carriage, Rane, then I'd like another one of her coming up the steps,' Leo directed, and the work began. Jack handed Shelley to the carriage with a gallantry that spoke volumes for his pleasure in the task, then went back with obvious reluctance to hold the horses' heads, while Shelley posed beside the carriage door.

'Will this do?'

'Beautifully.'

The brisk wind joined in and floated the veil in a gossamer cloud about Shelley's head. The black polished coachwork did its part and reflected the back view of the dress like a mirror, and Rane aimed her camera at its front. The delicate, heart-shaped neckline, the tight bodice and sleeves encrusted with tiny seed pearls, and the skirt, cascading from a tight waist in tiers of white lace to her feet—it was grace. It was magic. It was a fairy tale come true. It was a dress made especially for a bride who was just nineteen.

Rane's eyes blurred. Her fingers pressed the shutter button, and her voice issued automatic directions to Shelley. 'Turn to one side a little. No, slightly to the left. That's better, I can get the train in the picture now.' Her mind worked with its usual professional discipline, while her undisciplined heart felt as if it was about to break in two.

'It's a masterpiece, Leo. I knew you could do it.' Rane's voice came out husky, but her praise for the young designer's brilliance was as warm as it was sincere. 'That's the lot, Shelley.' She closed her camera and prepared to remove the film.

'Marion will be a bride in a million when she wears this,' Shelley said in an audible aside as she joined Rane at the top of the steps.

'By the time Marion becomes a bride, the dress will be old-fashioned.' Greville had overheard the mannequin's remark, and his voice as he answered was as icy as the wind. 'She can't marry anyone,' he emphasised the 'anyone' with a forbidding look at Leo, 'she can't marry anyone until she's twenty-one.'

'In law, she can marry at eighteen if she chooses,' Leo disputed hotly, and Rane caught a sharp breath.

'Don't try to retaliate, Leo,' her look begged him silently. 'Greville's too hard, too strong, for you.' But one glance at Leo's white face, the hot anger in his blue eyes, told her no plea could have any effect on him now. At last Greville had succeeded in goading him beyond endurance, and regardless of the consequences the young designer lost control of his temper and his tongue at the same time, and shouted back defiantly.

'Marion can marry at any time she chooses, without your consent!'

'As the law stands, she can,' Greville conceded with a shrug, and Rane stared at him suspiciously. Greville did not surrender. In tense silence she waited for the master stroke which was bound to come to crush the young Frenchman's resistance. 'As the law stands, she can,' Greville agreed smoothly, and added with deliberate slowness, 'but under the terms of her parents' will, if she marries before she becomes twenty-one she loses her inheritance.'

He played his master stroke. And Leo was not crushed. On the contrary, he seemed to be overjoyed at the revelation. His face lit up, and he actually laughed.

'Good!' he proclaimed loudly. 'In that case, Marion

and I will be married as soon as possible, with or without your consent.' He glowered at Greville, and in Rane's eyes he seemed to have suddenly matured. 'Marion won't need her inheritance,' he went on more quietly. 'When we're married, I'll provide for her, all she'll ever need,' he declared proudly, and Rane felt a swift stab of envy pierce through her like a pain. Lucky Marion. . . . 'That way,' Leo went on, 'no one will ever be able to accuse me of fortune-hunting!' And without waiting for Greville to reply, he turned on his heel and stamped indoors.

'If Leo continues to design dresses of this calibre,' Shelley remarked drily into the speaking silence that followed his departure, 'Marion's not likely to ever need her inheritance.'

Certainly the prospect did not appear to trouble the girl as she joined in the bustle of packing the Summer Collection, ready to return with it to Paris.

'Leo's chartered a plane to take everything back at once, including us.' Marion paused for a moment and rumpled her hand through her fair hair.

'I see you're wearing your ring,' Rane commented, catching sight of a flash of brilliant blue and white on her finger.

'I'll never be so careless with it again,' Marion replied ruefully. 'I'd hate to lose it, it belonged to my mother.'

'I thought Greville gave it to you for a birthday present?'

'Oh no, Greville was only the messenger, so to speak.' Marion fingered her ring gently. 'I'm to have a piece of Mother's jewellery every year on my birthday until eventually I have all of it. Greville gave me a course of driving lessons as his birthday present,' she added matter-of-factly.

So Greville had not attempted to eclipse Leo, after

all. Rane made a surprised mental adjustment in his favour, but before she had time to consider it Marion went on.

'I'm afraid with all this load of stuff, there won't be room for you in the chartered plane, but Greville's promised to take you with him in his jet.'

'I'm not coming to Paris with you,' Rane protested. 'My work's finished now I've photographed the wedding dress.'

'But you must come to my birthday party,' Marion insisted. 'You said you'd take photographs of my birthday cake and so on. Please, Rane, you promised,' she begged, and added, 'besides, you mustn't miss the showing of the Summer Collection. You must be there with us, to witness Leo's success.'

'With the wedding dress as his showpiece, the Collection should be a triumph,' Rane declared proudly, and registered the fact that if Greville intended to take her to Paris with him, he must intend to join the birthday party himself. Surely he was not also going to attend the showing of Leo's Collection?

'We're having the party in the salon after the showing,' Marion answered her unspoken question. 'Greville's got tickets for both of you.'

Rane gave up. Greville was totally unpredictable. She got ready for the flight in a state of numb acceptance. She felt like a puppet being manipulated by hidden strings, as she changed into the jade wool coat and skirt and tan cashmere sweater in which she arrived at Fullcote Hall, wondering if she was dreaming, and would soon wake up in her bedroom and open her eyes to the sight of Greville's daffodils.

The roar of the jet engines was reality, not a dream, and the daffodils faded below the plane in a yellow blur as they took off smoothly from the park and circled the Hall once, then set course for France.

'Now we can talk.' Greville left his seat in the cockpit and joined Rane in the comfortably furnished cabin of the plane, and she looked up at him fearfully.

'What are you doing back here?' Her voice rose in a frightened squeak. 'You're supposed to be driving the machine!'

'Don't panic,' Greville laughed easily. 'I've engaged the automatic pilot. It'll take charge for long enough to give you and me time to talk.'

'We can talk when we reach the ground,' Rane objected nervously, and felt her pulse begin to race. Greville safely up front, piloting the plane, was one thing. Greville in the cabin along with her, determined to have a tête-à-tête, was a complication with made her more nervous than having no visible pilot in the cockpit.

'This is the only place where I can be sure we shan't be interrupted,' he retorted, and calmly sat down beside her. 'You still hadn't answered me when Shelley interrupted us in the drawing room,' he reminded her unexpectedly.

'I've f-forgotten what we were t-talking about,' Rane stuttered untruthfully, edging nervously away from him.

'Shall I remind you?' His eyes rested on her flushed face, reading the changing expressions that flitted like light and shadow across her mobile features. Reading her very thoughts.

'Let's talk about Marion,' she countered breathlessly. 'And Leo.' She was on safer ground if she talked about Marion and Leo. 'Why don't you like him?' she sidetracked desperately.

'But I do,' Greville replied gravely, and Rane stared.

'But—he—you. . . .' She ground to an astonished halt.

'In fact,' Greville added for good measure, 'I thoroughly approve of Leo. Which is more than I've done of Marion's previous young men,' he finished drily.

'Then why . . .?' It was a day of revelations, and this one surpassed them all. 'You were absolutely beastly to Leo!' she accused him.

'I was beastly for a reason, Rane.' Greville reached out and put his arm around her and drew her across the seat to rest close against him, as if it was the most natural position in the world for her to be, and Rane went unresisting, too bemused by the swift turn of events to struggle against them—against Greville.

'I had to make sure of Leo,' Greville continued quietly when he had settled her to his satisfaction. 'I had to satisfy myself that he wanted Marion for the right reason.'

'Love?' she hazarded bravely, hardly daring to look up at him.

'Love,' he agreed solemnly, and the way he looked at her as he said it sent a thrilling warmth to thaw the ice that encased her heart. 'Other men have wooed Marion. Impecunious men, who saw in her a ready means to further their own ambitions.' The contempt in Greville's voice spoke volumes for his opinion of those other men.

'Leo loves Marion for herself,' Rane spoke up with courage and conviction. 'And she loves him, enough to give up her inheritance.'

'Marion won't lose her inheritance,' her guardian smiled at Rane's startled look.

'But you told Leo. . . .'

'I told Leo that Marion would lose her inheritance if she married before she reaches twenty-one. What I didn't tell him was that she'd only lose it if she marries *without my consent*, before she reaches twenty-one.'

'And you'll give your consent?' Rane sat bolt upright in the circle of his arms, her eyes bright with sudden hope. 'You will, won't you, Greville?' He nodded, and she exclaimed joyfully, 'How delighted they'll be! What a lovely birthday present for Marion!'

'A lovely *twenty-first* birthday present.' Gently Greville checked her eagerness. 'Until then it must remain our secret, Rane.' She thrilled to the 'our'. 'Just between you and me,' he insisted. 'Promise?'

'I promise.' She would promise much, much more, for Greville. She swallowed a quick ache in her throat and heard him say.

'Let Leo have the satisfaction of providing for his wife. Let him know the joy of achievement, and pride in his own success. Oh yes, I've no doubt he'll be a success,' his voice betrayed his respect for the young Frenchman's ability. 'By the time Marion reaches twenty-one, Leo will be wealthy enough himself not to resent her inheritance,' he said wisely. 'I don't want anything to come between them, and Marion's very young, she may not understand a man's pride, and Leo has plenty of that,' he approved.

'It's a lovely secret to take to their party,' she said joyfully.

'Do you think you can keep another secret, until tomorrow?'

Something in his look, in the way his arm tightened round her, sent a sweet flood of rose to warm her cheeks as he added, half teasing, wholly serious,

'You still haven't guessed why Zilla treated you so shamefully. No?' he relented as she shook her head, confused by the light that gleamed deep in his eyes, unable to answer because her heart was pounding so much that it took her breath away. 'Zilla could see, the whole world must have seen,' he laughed happily, 'that I love you, I need you, I want you.'

Rane had not seen, but it did not matter now. Greville's lips punctuated his words with a tender questing on her mouth, her eyes, along the soft, delicate line of her throat. 'I love you, Rane,' he groaned, and as if the admission broke the last barrier of his self-control he crushed her to him and buried his face in the soft copper gleams of her hair. 'I love you, I love you,' he murmured huskily, and when the ardour of his kisses prevented her from answering him, he took her head in both his hands and turned her face up to meet his.

'Tell me, don't keep me in suspense,' he begged. 'Is there any hope for me, Rane? Could you learn to love me, too?' he asked her brokenly.

'I do love you. I do.' It was a whisper, a tiny thread of sound, but it was enough. Her eyes shone, luminous with her love, her lips soft as the sweet breath of her confession, pressed like a vow upon his own.

'I do love you.' Eagerly she gave herself into his arms, her own rising to embrace him while her fingers played in the springy darkness of his hair. For long moments the plane droned unheeded across the sky, while they floated on their own cloud of ecstasy, discovering their love, until at last Rane lay back breathlessly against his shoulder, her eyes shining, and Greville confessed,

'I've been in torment all these weeks, not knowing. When I returned from Paris before Christmas, I couldn't get you out of my mind.'

'I kept your photograph,' she reminded him gently, and reached up tender fingers to smooth away the crease that the memory of the torment impressed between his eyes.

'That's what first gave me hope.' He captured her fingers and pressed his mouth to their soft tips. 'When I read your editor's note to say he'd found my photograph in your desk, and then the wind blew it towards the lake and you ran after it to save it, I tried to convince myself that it must mean something to you.'

'It meant everything to me. It was all I had. At least I could look at it now and then, because I didn't think you'd look at me, with all those gorgeous mannequins around you,' Rane remembered ruefully.

'Mannequins!' he grimaced. 'Lanky creatures who look as if they're in dire need of a good meal! I hope Leo will persuade Marion to give it up when they're married,' he frowned, and then his expression changed, and he laughed down at her, and teased wickedly, 'I'd rather have someone small and curvy. . . .' His glance ranged over her daintily rounded figure, and she dropped her lashes shyly and turned her face into his jacket to hide the rush of colour that stained her cheeks, saying in a muffled voice,

'Zilla thought you were falling in love with her.' Rane could feel sorry for Zilla, now.

'Zilla was in love with my diamond business.' Momentarily Greville's face hardened, then his expression cleared and he reached into his pocket. 'That reminds me,' he flipped open the lid of the small leather-covered box he brought out in his fingers. 'This arrived from our London showrooms this morning. Shall we see if it fits? I had to guess your size.'

'My size?' Rane raised her face from his jacket, and her eyes widened as they saw the ring in his fingers.

'Oh, Greville, it's beautiful!' she breathed ecstatically.

'You like it?' He had no need to ask. One look at the charmed expression on her face dispelled any doubts on that score. 'I said you should always choose emeralds, my darling,' he reminded her tenderly, and reaching down for her hand he slipped the ring on her engagement finger, and exclaimed his satisfaction, 'It's a perfect fit.'

'It's lovely, Greville.' She thanked him sweetly with murmuring lips that died into silence under the return pressure of his kiss.

'Do you recognise the diamonds?' he asked at last.

'No.' She regarded the gleaming stones flanking the brilliant centre emerald, one on either side. 'Is it . . .?'

'Our diamond. The crystal you photographed for me. You remember I said I had a destination in mind for the diamond?'

Rane believed he had meant quite a different destination, but wisely she forbore to tell him what that was, and asked instead,

'When shall we announce our engagement? It seems a shame to steal the limelight from Marion and Leo this afternoon.'

'Exactly what I thought,' Greville agreed with a smile, 'so we'll witness Leo's success, then go on to Marion's birthday party afterwards, and I thought this evening you and I would slip away and have dinner at Maxims, just the two of us, and announce our engagement tomorrow. In the meantime,' he waited for her happy nod before he rose reluctantly to his feet, 'in the meantime I'd better take charge up front, we'll be over Paris very soon.'

In what seemed to Rane no time at all they were in a taxi and making their way to the fashion salon, with the emerald and diamond ring once more back in its box and in Greville's pocket, awaiting the evening, their first, precious evening of a lifetime of evenings together.

'I knew Leo's Summer Collection would be a success, but this is absolutely fantastic!' Rane rose to her feet and clapped enthusiastically with the rest of the audience, and Greville stood as well, and clapped as hard as anybody, by her side. The applause went on and on, redoubling as Leo appeared, dressed in the blue velvet suit he reserved for occasions in the salon, to receive the congratulations that were his due, the delighted reception of an enthusiastic Press that ensured a brilliant future for the talented young designer.

'To Marion.'

At last the salon was cleared, and the birthday party was in full swing, and Greville called for silence to give the toast.

'To Marion.' He paused, and included with deliberation, 'and Leo.'

There was no doubt about his meaning, and he had a quick reward in the shining faces of the young couple.

'To Marion and Leo.'

Then Greville turned, with his glass still raised, and looked full on Rane, and the glow in his eyes added a toast that was meant for her alone.

'To us.'

Rane raised her glass and sipped, and over its rim her emerald eyes echoed, 'To us,' as she gazed back happily at Greville, no longer looking at the face of a stranger, but at the face of the man she loved.

ROMANCE

Next month's romances from Mills & Boon

Each month, you can choose from a world of variety in romance with Mills & Boon. These are the new titles to look out for next month.

FORGOTTEN PASSION Penny Jordan
DANGEROUS ENCOUNTER Flora Kidd
EVER AFTER Vanessa James
NEVER TOO LATE Betty Neels
THE LION ROCK Sally Wentworth
STORM IN THE NIGHT Margaret Pargeter
FALKONE'S PROMISE Rebecca Flanders
THE GATES OF RANGITATAU Robyn Donald
SERPENT IN PARADISE Rosemary Carter
REMEMBER ME, MY LOVE Valerie Parv
NO QUIET REFUGE Jessica Steele
FULL CIRCLE Rosemary Hammond

Buy them from your usual paperback stockist, or write to: Mills & Boon Reader Service, P.O. Box 236, Thornton Rd, Croydon, Surrey CR9 3RU, England. Readers in South Africa-write to: Mills & Boon Reader Service of Southern Africa, Private Bag X3010, Randburg, 2125.

Mills & Boon
the rose of romance

ROMANCE

Variety is the spice of romance

Each month, Mills & Boon publish new romances. New stories about people falling in love. A world of variety in romance – from the best writers in the romantic world. Choose from these titles in November.

CHAINS OF REGRET Margaret Pargeter
BELOVED STRANGER Elizabeth Oldfield
SUBTLE REVENGE Carole Mortimer
MARRIAGE UNDER FIRE Daphne Clair
A BAD ENEMY Sara Craven
SAVAGE ATONEMENT Penny Jordan
A SECRET INTIMACY Charlotte Lamb
GENTLE PERSUASION Claudia Jameson
THE FACE OF THE STRANGER Angela Carson
THE TYZAK INHERITANCE Nicola West
TETHERED LIBERTY Jessica Steele
NO OTHER CHANCE Avery Thorne

On sale where you buy paperbacks. If you require further information or have any difficulty obtaining them, write to: Mills & Boon Reader Service, PO Box 236, Thornton Road, Croydon, Surrey CR9 3RU, England.

Mills & Boon
the rose of romance